W9-BQS-900

# TROUBLE AT FISH CAMP

*Book Two in the Ways of the Williwaw Series*

SALLY BAIR

Sally Bair

abbott press®
A DIVISION OF WRITER'S DIGEST

**Trouble at Fish Camp**
**Book Two in the Ways of the Williwaw Series**



*Abbott Press books may be ordered through booksellers or by contacting:*

*Abbott Press*
*1663 Liberty Drive*
*Bloomington, IN 47403*
*www.abbottpress.com*
*Phone: 1-866-697-5310*



*Cover illustration by Devin Gage, dgage_7@hotmail.com*

*ISBN: 978-1-4582-0399-1 (sc)*
*ISBN: 978-1-4582-0398-4 (e)*

*Library of Congress Control Number: 2012909503*

*Printed in the United States of America*

*Abbott Press rev. date: 6/7/2012*

# ACKNOWLEDGMENTS

Thank you—

—Yarnspinners for your time and effort in critiquing "Trouble at Fish Camp"

—My faithful readers: Cherrie, Mikhael, Kayde, Ann, and Barb

—My church and prayer group for keeping me in prayer through the writing process

—Julie Lessman and Patti Lacy, my encouraging teachers of fiction at the Green Lake Christian Writers' Conference

# CONTENTS

*Chapter 1*

# THE BULLY

Freddy Schumaker's guts churned. If only he felt as peaceful as the soft waves coming into shore. The fish camp on Kodiak Island where he and his friend, Jake Bergren, sat mending nets was usually the most serene place in the world. But this summer, Freddy's cousin, Pete, was at the neighboring camp. That meant trouble. Not only was Pete a bully, he held a secret about Freddy that must not be told.

Freddy jerked his head around at the sound of a grunt. Shocked, he saw Jake lying on the gritty beach clutching his belly. Pete stood over him, a menacing sneer on his face.

"Lay off!" Freddy yelled. "Jake didn't do nothin' to you."

Pete turned away from Jake and glared. He balled up his fist and stepped to within a hair of Freddy's face. "He stole my job on the *Danny Boy*, that's what he did!" Pete shoved Freddy hard.

Freddy clenched his teeth, feeling his lip scar tighten. He charged into Pete, growling like a wounded bear, and grabbed his shirt. Buttons popped. Pete jerked back. They fell hard, sand spraying like birdshot. Pete grunted, squeezing Freddy's neck. Fear shot through Freddy. He yanked Pete's hands away with a strength he didn't know he possessed. "Run, Jake!" he croaked. "An' watch your back!"

Pete turned towards Jake. "Think you can show up here and act like nothing happened?" He yelled, his words spitting like hailstones. "Well, you got another think coming! You messed with me about that job … and I won't forget it."

Freddy's fists tightened. "Pete, don't threaten Jake."

"I'm not threatening. I'm promising."

Ready for another attack, Freddy dug into his jeans pocket for the lucky jackknife he always kept there. He crouched and held his breath. Could he actually hurt his cousin? No matter how mean he was?

Pete sneered and stepped away. The breath whooshed out of Freddy's aching lungs as he withdrew his hand from the knife. Relieved, he turned away. He knew he'd have to figure how to keep Jake safe from Pete's clutches.

*Can't have Pete wantin' to beat my buddy Jake to a pulp for somethin' that happened way last winter. I'm tired of bein' beat up by my stinkin' cousin. He's nothin' but a bully. It don't matter I'm almost nineteen and even though he's only fifteen, he's tougher than me. But I gotta try an' make him see reason.*

Heart still pounding, Freddy ran after Pete. "Hey, man. We're blood! So why the attitude? I told you before, Jake gettin' that job on the boat had nothin' to do with you. The skipper changed his plans, that's all. Wasn't Jake's fault. Besides, that was months ago." Freddy held his breath and waited for another punch. His fingers curled around the jackknife again.

Pete cracked his knuckles and spit on the sand as he kept walking towards his dad's cabin around the tip of Eagle Point. "Don't think just 'cuz you're my cousin, I'll go easy on you. You're the one who brought Jake here. You both better watch your backs."

Relieved Pete wasn't going to punch him again, Freddy still couldn't shake his nervousness about what could happen next. He dragged himself back to Sitting Rock where he and Jake had to finish mending nets. He felt tired, drained to his toenails. As if he'd swum ten miles. *This won't get any easier. Tomorrow's the opener of salmon fishing and I'll be even more tired. Can't tell what Pete's gonna do next. No wonder he keeps me on edge.*

But now the set-nets had to be mended. He plunked his tired body down on the rock. Not hard work, just monotonous and never-ending. A part of life for all fishermen in this Land of the Midnight Sun. He picked up his long mending needle and started mending net holes. But he found it hard to concentrate.

Looking out across the water from Eagle Point fish camp on the southwest shore of Kodiak, Freddy tried to forget about Pete. He faced the spot across Shelikof Straight where their crab boat had gone down last December. He'd never forget that day. Violent winds—williwaws—coming off the Alaska Peninsula had built to 100 knots. Between the wind and sixteen-foot seas, the *Danny Boy,* their seventy-two-foot fishing vessel, didn't have a chance. Down she went, almost taking the crew of five with her.

*We were headin' for dead even with our survival suits on. Thought we'd never get the ice off that life raft.* Freddy shivered, thinking about their close call.

Miraculously, the skipper's Mayday call had reached the Coast Guard station before the boat's navigation system quit. A Coast Guard swimmer plucked Freddy and the others out one by one, like orange fishing bobbers, from their flooding life raft.

Freddy couldn't stop thinking about their rescue. *My guts still churn when I picture us jumpin' into that flimsy raft. Pitchin' and bobbin' just like the Danny Boy before the sea swallowed her whole.*

It turned out okay, though. Freddy chuckled, remembering how his friend got religion over their near-disaster. *Maybe Jake's right when he says God saved us. He changed from a fightin', greenhorn kid with an attitude to a religious fanatic. Not that it makes me think less of him. Even though his preachin' gets tiresome at times.* Freddy chuckled again.

"What's so funny?" Jake asked, his mending needle poised heavenward. He shook his head free of the remaining sand that had gathered there when Pete had thrown him to the ground. "Your cousin's a bully and you're laughing?" He punched Freddy on the arm.

"Naw, it's not that. Just thinkin' 'bout our 'disaster at sea,' as you call it."

Jake snorted. "Yeah, some ending to our crabbing trip. But … seriously, what are we going to do about Pete? He's a mean one. Does he hold grudges for long?"

Freddy remained quiet. He and Pete had their own history. How could he answer Jake's question? It had been eight years since Freddy had almost let his little sister, Mattie, drown and Pete had seen it happen. Even though Pete had never said a word about it, he kept threatening to. Freddy just knew if Pete got mad enough, he'd think nothing of using the awful secret as a weapon. Then everyone would hate him. Jake wouldn't want to be his friend any more if he knew. Neither would Jake's sister, Joanie, whom he had met just this week.

Freddy already liked Joanie's spunky attitude. Reminded him of his sisters. He was glad she had come with Jake to fish camp. Their boss and owner of the camp, Bernie and his wife, Barb, had hired Joanie to babysit Jessica, their two-year-old daughter, during the salmon fishing season.

*No, I can't say a word to nobody. I'll just hafta try not to get Pete riled up any more than he is. It'll be like walkin' on eggs again. Like Ma and the girls and I did before Dad left. Good riddance to the drunken deadbeat."*

"What're you mumbling about? I just asked you a simple question."

Freddy jerked his head up. "Uh, sorry. Yeah, Pete does hold grudges. You gotta be extra careful around him." He forced a crooked smile across his face and whacked Jake on the back. "But we don't hafta be around him much. Not to worry."

Jake grunted, following it with a loud sigh. "Remember how seasick I got on the way out to the fishing grounds? Well, the water may be calmer here …" he pointed towards the ocean waves "… but my muscles tense just thinking about Pete's bullying." Jake turned to face Freddy. "This is my problem, though. You shouldn't have to take the brunt of his anger. Let me handle it."

Freddy laughed. "Yeah, right. Remember on the boat last year? How you staggered up the steps to the wheelhouse an' slipped on the deck and puked from seasickness? If Pete gets ahold of you alone, you'll be staggerin' the same way. Maybe pukin', too."

Freddy whirled around at the sound of someone approaching. "Hey! Here's your little sister, Jake!" He jumped up to help Joanie as she limped down the hill. "Here, Little Sis, let me take your color crayons."

"Ha! I can do it myself. And Freddy," Joanie said, hands on hips when she reached the Sitting Rock with the help of her cane, "when are you gonna stop your bad grammar? Oh, no!" she giggled. "You've got me doing it, too. Besides, I'm not Jake's *little* sister. I may be only fifteen, but I'm tough. Aren't I, Jake?" She batted her eyelashes and flexed her biceps at her brother.

Jake laughed. "Right, Joanie. Especially since your accident. You're not the female jock you used to be, you know."

"Hey, Bro! You're supposed to show your friend I'm tough, not a wimp," Joanie scolded. "So I use a cane. So what? It wasn't that long ago I sat in a wheelchair, remember? I'm praying I'll walk without this cane some day, too. Besides, I'm tough in other ways, so there."

"Hey, Little Sis," Freddy said. "Let's get back to this grammar thing. You hardly know me, and already you criticize my grammar? 'Sides, how do you know if I talk this way all the time?"

"Trust me, you do." Joanie's eyes twinkled. "Actually, I didn't come down here to correct your grammar …yet. I came to sketch while Jessica takes a nap. And for your information, I don't use color crayons. I'm not a little kid. I use pencils and charcoal. Barb said I could take a break from babysitting. So here I am."

Joanie set up her easel. "How about you and me making a deal, Fred?"

"Freddy's my name, fishin's my game. So … what's your deal, Little Sis?"

Joanie rolled her eyes. "Joanie's my name, drawing's my game. So there." She swung her blond ponytail near his face. "Okay, here's the deal, Fred-dy. You teach me about the flora and fauna around camp and I'll teach you better grammar. Deal?" She held out her hand.

Freddy backed up as if he'd touched a hot iron. With mock shock, he blurted, "Flora and fauna? Say whatcha mean. You *do* mean flowers and critters, don'tcha? An' besides, think I'd have a little girl teach me somethin'? Not in a blue moon! An' my grammar ain't that bad nohow."

Joanie laughed and then became serious. "I'll stop calling you Fred if you stop calling me Little Sis. By the way, your grammar is atrocious. But you have great potential. You don't want it to go to waste, do you? I can see it already. You'd make a great teacher some day. I've seen how you …"

Freddy's heart skipped with surprise—and hope. Hadn't he always loved teaching his little sisters how to do things?

"… how you showed Jake how to mend nets, Fred," Joanie said. "He also told me if it hadn't been for you, he would have had a harder time learning about all the ropes on board the *Danny Boy* and …."

"Lines, Joanie. Not ropes. Cowboys use ropes. Fisherfolk use lines."

"See? That proves you'd make a great teacher."

Not ready to give in, Freddy mumbled, "I'll think about it," and returned to his mending, holding up a large section of a net that was shredded.

"Wow, that's some hole!" Jake said. "Guess that'll take you a while to mend, huh? So what do you think happened to it?"

"Prob'ly it got too close to the bottom and the tide dragged it back an' forth along the rocks. Or on the coal."

"Coal?"

"Yeah, there's lots of coal deposits up in this country. Didn'tcha know? People walk along the beach an' pick up what the tide washes ashore. They use it to heat their cabins."

Joanie grinned as she set up her portable easel and sketch pad and started to draw the scene before her. "Like I said, Fred. You're a born teacher."

While Freddy mended the shredded net, he glanced over at the sketches Joanie was drawing of the ocean and shore. "Not bad, Little Sis. Where'd you learn to draw?"

"Back in Wisconsin where we went to school … Jake told you we grew up by Lake Superior, didn't he?"

"Yeah, he said somethin' about it. You moved to Anchorage when?"

"Three years ago," Joanie said. "The school let Jake and me skip a grade."

"How'd that happen?"

With an air of pride, Joanie raised her nose in the air. "I'm a successful product of the Wisconsin public school system, that's how." Her eyes sparkled.

Freddy snorted. "Yeah, right. So … do you like Alaska?"

"I do. Except I'm not used to the long daylight hours in summer. I still hardly believe I can sit outside at eleven at night and it's still light out. I miss the big lake, too. It doesn't have williwaws or tricky tides like the Pacific, but it's big and beautiful—and cold, of course."

Freddy turned his head when he heard a familiar voice behind them. "Uh-oh, here's trouble again," he whispered. Ignoring his fear, Freddy jumped up and stepped in front of Joanie. "Whaddaya want now, Pete?"

Pete bent over, howling with malicious laughter. "So you've turned into a protector of cripples, huh, freaky cousin?"

Freddy bristled. "Leave her alone! An' don't call me a freak! Go back to your work." Without realizing, Freddy touched the scar on his lip. Ever since his harelip surgery as a child, he'd hated the word freak. Because he felt like one.

"Ain't you s'posed to be helpin' your dad? Or are you slackin' off again?"

Pete's face turned purple. "None of your business! But ..." he turned to Joanie with a smirk, "... *this* little girl is slacking off, I'm thinking. So what're you doing, little girl? Where's the baby you're supposed to be watching?"

Joanie straightened and faced her tormentor. "None of *your* business, Nosy! And what is it with you guys calling me a little girl? I'm just as strong as ..."

Pete swung his arm forward, knocking Joanie's easel to the sand. "Let's see you pick it up, Crippy." He stalked off, again cracking his knuckles. With a backward glance, he shouted, "Hey, Freddy, I'd stay away from her if I were you. She might go after you with her cane. But be sure to tell her you're a baby killer."

Freddy's heart beat double time. He fingered the knife in his pocket as he began following his cousin. "You're in for it now, you bully!" Withdrawing his empty hand, he lunged for Pete, who sidestepped.

"Freddy, don't!" Joanie's desperate cry brought him to a halt. Pete turned to give them a dirty look and then continued to his cabin, laughing all the way.

By the time Joanie had retrieved her drawing equipment, Freddy was back at Sitting Rock. His legs still shook as he collapsed onto the rock. He took the closed knife out of his pocket and rolled it back and forth in his palm.

"So what's with the knife?" Jake's mouth drew into a tight line.

Freddy opened it, held it out. "My lucky knife, Jake. Remember? I used it to cut our raft free from the *Danny Boy.* Just in time, too."

"Well, don't go using it around here. Somebody could get hurt."

"So what's up with Pete, Fred?" Joanie asked. "And why did he call you a baby killer?" Joanie's gaze pierced him through and through.

"Aw, nothin'. He's full of crap. I ain't no killer." Freddy closed his knife and shoved it back into his pocket.

"Your cousin's got a problem," Jake muttered.

*Whew! Dodged the bullet that time. Maybe Joanie'll take my word for it and forget what Pete said to me.*

Silence settled among the three young people. Except for the relentless swishing of water onto the beach, the only sound came from Joanie's sudden, furious pencil strokes across her sketch pad. Finally she ripped a piece of paper from the pad and thrust it in front of their faces. "Notice something shocking?" Her face was serious as she moved the drawing with shaking hands towards their faces, back and forth, like a cobra's undulating head enticing its victim.

*Chapter 2*

# THE SKETCH

Jake's intake of breath matched Freddy's surprise at the likeness Joanie had drawn of Pete. Freddy could have sworn it was Jake in the picture. Then he remembered something. "Hey, Jake! Didn't you tell me you were adopted? Maybe Pete's your brother. Ha-ha." Freddy's nervous laugh floated over the rippling ocean waves.

"Yeah, right," Jake spat out. "If he was, I'd never claim him. Besides, don't they say everyone has a likeness somewhere in the world? Yeah, that's it. He's my 'twin.'" But Jake didn't sound convincing to Freddy.

Joanie nodded, a look of doubt on her face. "You're right, Bro. He's just your twin. But … the hair line and coloring are identical. And you have the same bulky build. Hm-m. Maybe he was a high school wrestler like you, Jake."

Freddy's cackle turned their heads. "Not unless he wrestled in juvie. That's where he was last year."

"Juvie?" Joanie asked.

"Yeah. You know. Juvenile prison.

"Oh, right. Seriously? He spent time there?"

"Almost broke his dad's heart, too," Freddy said.

"I can imagine," Jake added. "I haven't met his dad yet. What's his name again?"

"Harold. They call him Hal. Nicest uncle I could ever have. A little too easy on Pete, though. He spoils him. 'Specially since Pete's mom died. Pete don't deserve spoilin'. Pete don't deserve much of ..."

"Doesn't."

"Huh?"

Joanie smiled. "Pete *doesn't* deserve much. Come on, Fred, get with the act. Bad grammar won't take you anywhere. I'll teach you. Whenever you're ready, the opportunity is yours."

"Yeah, and I s'pose I'd hafta learn all them big words you use, too."

"All *those* big words, not *them*. And no, your vocabulary is fine. It's just your atrocious grammar that needs fixing."

"There you go again." Freddy shook his head.

*Maybe it wouldn't hurt to get some better learnin'. Sure didn't in school, the way the kids tore into me about my scar. Ain't my fault the doc botched my harelip surgery. Funny, but Joanie ain't said nothin' 'bout my scar. I'll hafta make sure, though, that she don't find out what I did … or almost did to my sister Mattie. She'd blackball me forever. Joanie's cute. Reminds me of Mattie an' Merry. Reminds me that I miss my little sisters.*

"Maybe I'll think on it, Little Sis."

When Jake cleared his throat, Freddy looked up at him. "Hey, man! You're as pale as a boat lost in the fog. What's wrong? You don't *really* think Pete's your brother, do you?"

Jake tightened his lips. He shook his head but his lips quivered. "Quit your daydreaming, Freddy. We have to finish mending these nets or Bernie'll be on our tails. Tomorrow's opening day of salmon fishing, don't forget."

"Yep. Price is good, too, for the first opener. Sure hope the Fish and Game keep it open for a long time. Don't like them … er, *those* closures much. They give us catch-up time for repairs an' stuff, but no money."

Joanie clapped. "Yay, Fred! You got the right word. By the way, since you're the … ahem, teacher among us, explain openers and closures. I never did learn about it in school."

Chuckling, Freddy poked her in the arm. "That's 'cuz you're a city girl. Well, you see, the Alaska Department of Fish and Game hire people to count the salmon goin' through their weirs at the mouth of certain rivers. Their count shows how many salmon are runnin', an' that's when they give us fishermen the go-ahead to fish with our set-nets. When the count goes down, they set a closure. That stops all fishin'. Sometimes it's for twenty-four hours, sometimes longer."

Joanie ribbed Freddy lightly. "See, I told you. You can teach! And now that I know about openers and closures, I'll pray there are few closures because I know you all need the money."

*There she goes prayin' again. Just 'cuz her dad's a chaplain.* Freddy sighed dramatically. "As if God could turn on a faucet to let the fish slow or speed up. It don't happen that way."

"*Doesn't,* Fred, not *don't.* And you're wrong. He can turn on any faucet He wants. After all, He's almighty. Right, Jake?" Joanie gave her brother a playful slap.

"Yep. Whether you like it or not, Freddy," Jake added. "Time you gave some serious thought to the Almighty. You're avoiding the issue. I can see it in your eyes."

Freddy studied his boots. *If they only knew. God wouldn't want me nohow. Not after what I did. I can still see Mattie's floating form in that swimmin' pool, all limp and lookin' dead. I really blew it. Shouldn'ta watched Pete do them wheelies, showin' off on his new bike like he did. Ma was right. I shoulda been watchin' Mattie closer. I let her down. Even though I was just a kid myself, I shoulda known better. Nope, God don't want nothin' to do with a loser like me.*

"Hey! You're daydreaming again." Jake shook Freddy's arm. "We didn't mean to put you in a slump. I don't know what it's about, but it's time to pay attention to this mending."

Relieved, Freddy rejoined his friend in patching holes in the large set-net while Joanie sketched more scenes around them. He sneaked a peak at her drawing. "You're good, Little Sis. When I have time, I'll show you some bee-yoo-tee-ful wildflowers up in the hills. While you draw, you can learn me some more grammar."

Joanie grimaced, but her eyes sparkled as she nodded her head vigorously. "It's a deal, Fred. I can hardly wait." She held out her hand. "Put 'er there, partner."

Freddy shook her hand. "Jist be sure Pete don't … *doesn't* find out or he'll make both our lives miserable. More miserable than ever, that is. Jake, you better promise, too."

Both agreed with enthusiasm. A grin split Jake's face. "Leave it to Joanie to make a teacher out of you."

Freddy's mood lightened as they bantered back and forth. Maybe this summer wouldn't be so bad after all. In spite of Pete's threats and bullying. In spite of his two friends' religious talk. In spite of trying to keep his past hidden. *If they find out, they'll hate me. Much as I'd like to throttle Pete, I don't dare. Can't take the chance he'll tell on me. But how can I stay on his good side when he's such a jerk?*

Freddy paused in his work, his thoughts returning to that fateful day. Mattie, only five years old, had wanted to go swimming at the neighborhood pool, even if it was after closing hours.

"Please, Mama? It's so hot out. Freddy will stay with me every second … won't you, Freddy?" She had pleaded until their mother grew tired of the whining and gave in.

Freddy never forgot her warning. "If anything happens to Mattie, I'll disown you."

More memories rushed in. Memories tattooed forever on his mind. Pete's grinning face turning to shock … Freddy jolting around, seeing Mattie lying face down in the deep end … jumping in … lifting her lifeless body to poolside … pumping her chest until water and vomit spewed out of her mouth … listening for her cough, which came after an eternity … tears running down his cheeks … his choking voice screaming to Pete to call 911, making Pete promise never to tell on him … Mattie lying in the ER. His mom had watched Mattie for days, looking for signs of brain damage. When none showed up, Freddie's sense of relief still couldn't erase his feeling of guilt.

Freddy took a deep breath to clear his head. He jumped up from Sitting Rock. "Let's head back to the cabin, Jake. Time to eat."

"What's with you, man? You look rough." Jake's obvious concern brought Freddy to his senses.

"Nothin's wrong. I'm fine." He faked a laugh. "Let's just go. I'm hungry. Come on, Joanie. I'll carry your easel an' stuff."

The three trudged uphill silently. Freddy, in the lead, swallowed the lump in his throat, trying hard to forget the day he nearly let his sister drown.

## Chapter 3

# A BEAR SCARE

"Mm-m, somethin' smells good." Freddy broke the fragile silence as they reached their boss's crude cabin. They sat around the square table where Bernie took a chair next to Jessica, who plunked a toy against her high chair tray. Barb dished up heaping bowls of food.

Freddy remembered that Jake's parents would be coming for a visit from Anchorage in a week or so. Where would everyone sit then? He speared a forkful of food. "Barb, you're a good cook."

Jake agreed. "Sure beats the terrible meals on the *Danny Boy,* huh, Freddy? Always on the run, we ate more junk food than a bear digging at the dump. A wonder we survived." His smirk reached Freddy's gaze. "At least we had lots of carbs to fuel our energy ... like cookies and Ramen noodles."

Everyone laughed as Barb passed her homemade Italian spaghetti and French bread around the table. A full bowl of fresh salad followed. Freddy and Jake stuffed themselves and then suggested a game of Monopoly. Halfway through the long game, Jake started to nod off.

Bernie chuckled. "Put in a hard day's work, Jake?"

Freddy hooted. But he too couldn't wait to go to bed.

Joanie poked her brother's ribs. "Yeah, all that time spent on Sitting Rock will do it every time. To say nothing about the skirmishes you guys faced."

The adults gave her a puzzled look. Freddy felt his face heat up and quickly said, "I think I'm as tired as he is after that big meal."

Jake cleared his throat. "I'm just not used to eating so much good food at one time. Being in college last semester, I didn't eat much. Barb, your meals sure beat cafeteria food. I agree with Freddy. That was a great meal. Reminds me of my mom's cooking."

Bernie grinned as though he had cooked the meal himself. "Well, I guess you boys should hit the hay," he said. "Tomorrow's a big day. Long and hard."

Freddy sighed in relief that the grown-ups hadn't asked about the "skirmishes." He didn't want them to know and he knew Jake didn't want them to, either.

Even though it was still light out, he and Jake headed to their eight-by-eight tent in the yard. Freddy flopped down on his sleeping bag among a mess of stuff.

"How can you find anything in this pigpen … your half, that is?" Jake asked. "Reminds me of your bunk on the *Danny Boy.* Smells almost as bad, too."

"So what? I know where my stuff is. That's all that matters."

Jake made a flying landing on Freddy's back, surprising him into a grunt.

"I'll teach you," Freddy said, a chuckle escaping his scarred lip. He pinned Jake's legs with his own in a wrestling hold, fighting to throw Jake off. With one last hard squeeze to Jake's chest, Freddy let go.

Jake flopped over to his sleeping bag, still laughing. "I'll win a round with you yet. I'm bigger than you."

"Yeah, right. So how come I won when we arm wrestled on the *Danny Boy*?"

Turning to the tent wall, Jake yawned then mumbled, "Still too weak from seasickness. Remember?"

In seconds he was sleeping. As Freddy listened to Jake's rhythmic breathing, he thought back to their arm wrestling match. *Can't believe I won the match, with him bein' so bulky and a wrestlin' champ in high school, too. I may be skinny, but guess my muscles can still beat his.*

Freddy jerked at a sudden noise outside. He reached over and gave Jake's arm a good shake. "Wake up! There's a bear outside."

Jake sat straight up. "Can't be," he mumbled. "Bernie said bears don't come near this barren part of the island."

"Well, they do now. I'm sure it was a bear."

"Aw, go back to sleep. Maybe it was a fox." Jake turned on his side to face the tent wall again. Soon his snores filled the tent.

Sleep didn't come easily for Freddy. Positive a bear had come by, he kept waiting to hear more, kept listening for another noise. He began worrying about Kodiak bears walking about, getting too close to Joanie and Jessica, let alone the rest of them. *I'll have to watch extra careful-like when anyone goes outside the cabin.* His eyes grew heavy ….

Next thing he knew, Bernie's cowbell and shout woke him. "Six o'clock, boys. Time to go fishing."

Muttering, Freddy peeked outside the tent. No bears. He'd look for tracks later. The mid-May sun, up for eighteen hours a day by now, shone brightly across the water. *Am I ready for this salmon season? Here I'm just startin', and already tired. Shouldn't've spent so much time worryin' last night.*

"What did you say, Freddy?"

"Oh, nothin'. Just not awake yet. But I know I heard a bear last night." Freddy threw on the same clothes he'd worn the day before.

Jake chuckled. "Not a chance. But if you want, tell Bernie. And by the way, clean up your half of the tent before we go eat. It's repulsive!"

In a snit, Freddy ignored him and stomped into the cabin for breakfast. "Bernie, I heard a bear last night."

Bernie and Barb laughed. "No way," Bernie said. "Aren't any bears around here. You must have heard a red fox."

"That's what Jake said. But I heard it huff. Let's go look for tracks. I'll prove it."

Bernie sighed, but followed Freddy to the tent. "Let's hurry, I'm hungry."

After inspecting the area around the tent, Bernie said, "Can't see any tracks, Freddy. Sorry." He started back just as Jake emerged from the tent.

"Wait! Here!" Freddy pulled on Bernie's sleeve. "See how the grass is bent over? A fox wouldn't've made that big a print. That deep a one, neither. And see how far apart they are? Gotta been a bear."

"Hm-m." Bernie peered at the trampled grass areas. "Hasn't been a brown bear around these parts for years. Do you have food in your tent? Better get rid of it, in case it was a bear. Even if it was a red fox, you don't want to accidentally corner any kind of critter in your tent."

Jake looked at Freddy. "Hear that? Hard to tell what you've got hiding in that mess of yours. Candy? Snacks? Or you-know-what?"

Freddy's eyes become slits as he gave Jake a hard look. *He's still thinkin' about that secret stash of pot I had on the boat. I don't do that no more, though. I better tell him.*

Back at the cabin, Bernie finished his coffee. "Just in case, I'll give the authorities a ring. To let them know. Not that they can do much except keep a close eye on the bear. But, hey, it's time to eat first."

After finishing breakfast, Bernie put in a call to the Alaska Department of Fish and Game on the CB radio then turned to Freddy and Jake. "Okay, boys, time to get out there and catch some salmon."

He grabbed three orange float coats, tossing one each to them, along with pairs of cotton gloves. He pointed to some rubberized, bib rain pants hanging behind the cabin door and then took off down the hill to the skiff. Hidden from cabin view, it sat protected from the surf around the sharp point of land where the boys had sat mending nets the day before.

Freddy and Jake climbed into their bibs, slipped on the float coats, and followed Bernie to the skiff. Freddy touched Jake's shoulder. "These float coats is called body markers, you know."

Jake looked up, surprise clouding his face.

"Yep. Them's not warm enough to keep you from hypothermia. So if you're alone and you fall in the drink, your coat'll keep you up, but you'll freeze to death before you reach your boat."

Jake shuddered. "You sure have a way of scaring me. Like the plenty of times you tried on the *Danny Boy.*"

Looking out at the open water, Freddy watched Bernie's other boat, a brand-new holding skiff, bob up and down in the waves. The waves were nothing like the williwaws they'd encountered, but still … he knew that northern Pacific water could be rough anywhere.

Bernie and Freddy had anchored the holding skiff earlier, before Jake arrived at camp. After fishing from the smaller skiff, they would transfer their catch to the holding skiff until an attending boat, called a tender, came by to transfer and weigh their fish. The tender would then transport the fish to the cannery in the city of Kodiak.

"Oof! This surf is heavy," Jake groaned as he helped push the skiff out from its protected vantage point.

Freddy groaned, too. "Yeah, the tide's comin' in fast now. Shoulda waited a few hours, huh, Bernie? Then I coulda slept longer." He wiggled his eyebrows at his boss.

"Uh-huh. Thought you wanted to make money this summer, Freddy. Can't do that while you're waiting for the tide. That's a fact."

"Just kiddin', Boss," Freddy joked. Once he and Jake freed the skiff from the beach's sandy bottom into the frothy waves, they jumped into it while Bernie held it steady. Bernie followed and then grabbed the throttle to start the motor.

Bernie mumbled, "Forgot to hook a running line from shore to the skiff. Got to do that later."

Freddy looked up at Jake. "The boss means that then the skiff can stay out in the water a little ways, away from the sand and surf. But it also means our feet might get wet wadin' out to the skiff. Just somethin' we'll hafta get used to once Bernie hooks the line. Our work'll be easier … but wetter. "

As they motored out, Freddy focused on the shoreline. *That scraggly, old cottonwood standin' alone up there on the hill … my favorite spot. Wonder how many more years it'll last. 'Cept for willows 'n' alders along the crick, it's the only tree around on this here tundra. Wonder if the eagles are nesting there again.* Freddy studied the short grass covering the hill, knowing it would grow much higher as summer progressed.

He reveled in the warmth of his float coat with its foam sleeves and a foam vest. But his face and ears felt cold from the wind.

"What's the temp, Boss?" Freddy hunched over as they motored to the nearest buoy a couple hundred yards from shore.

"I'd say around 44. You already forget how cold Alaska can be in early June? Don't worry, you won't even notice the chilly mornings once you get back into the routine. Like you did last summer." He smirked at Freddy and Jake. "Unless either of you falls in, of course."

Jake's eyes twinkled. "Not me, Boss. Freddy, maybe. But I guess we both had enough of that to last us seven lifetimes."

Freddy looked puzzled. "Why seven? I don't get it."

Jake blushed. "Oops. Didn't mean to say that. Guess my dad's religious teaching kind of got in the way of my head. See, he once told me that seven is a common biblical number. It means complete. Final. Yeah, that's it. Final. And that's what I want my hands-on … pardon my pun … ocean water experience to be. Final."

Bernie and Freddy roared, their hearty laughter carrying on the wind as they approached the first buoy.

*Chapter 4*

# PICKING FISH

The three fishermen worked hard attaching the mended nets to the lines which already had been set. They hooked one end of the first net to a large, offshore rock that had holes bored into it and the other end to permanent anchors that were attached to buoys. The top of the net was tied to the buoys and the bottom to the anchors. The men repeated the process with the second net set about a fifth of a mile away.

"I'm curious," Jake said. "How do these nets work, anyway? It's a darn sight different from using crab pots on the Bering Sea."

Freddy chuckled. "Yeah, you city boys don't know nothin' about real fishin', do you?" He held up one long side of a net. "See these corks? They float on top of the water." He held up part of the other length. "See this thin line of lead on the bottom? That keeps this side of the net down. But it shouldn't touch the bottom where there are rocks. If the lead line gets on the bottom, it gets tangled on debris and bottom fish. And crabs and sculpins and Irish lords. Got it?"

Jake nodded. "Yeah, I can picture the net standing like a vertical curtain in the water. Its length must spread in an arc across the water surface. As the tide moves it. Right?"

"Right. And they're seventy-five fathoms each," Bernie said. "That's four-hundred fifty feet long. Longer than a football field. Enough to trap lots of big reds."

Jake whistled. "And what kind of anchors hold the nets down?"

Bernie laughed. "Keep telling him, Teach." He slapped Freddy on the back.

"They ain't much, Jake. Some bags of rocks tied up with old netting is all."

"Are you serious? That's all? Well, then tell me this. Why don't we fish for King salmon?"

"Kings ain't … aren't common around Kodiak," Freddy explained. "They're fished mostly in Cook Inlet 'n' along the southeast coast. You already know that red salmon are called sockeyes and aren't as big as kings. But reds are still the most valuable salmon in this part of the Pacific … pay the most bucks. An' there's more of 'em. 'Bout ninety percent of our catch will be reds."

"I know I like the taste of red salmon better than others," Jake said, "but what makes them better? And higher priced?"

Freddy shrugged. "It's debatable. Some say they taste better, some say they look better. Guess it's a matter of choice. I do know they have a higher oil content than other species." He grinned at Jake. "You're full of questions today, aren't you?"

"I'm just curious. Joanie's right. You're a good teacher." Jake inspected the net closer as he spoke.

Not used to compliments, Freddy felt his face heat up. "Yeah, well, anyway … see this piece o' braided line strung along each side? It holds the corks along the top line and the lead along the bottom line. The lead is threaded right into the braided line here … like this." He also pointed to the seven-inch corks that were threaded every three to six feet apart on the top line.

"These nets are heavy. Must weigh a couple hundred pounds. Right?" Jake asked.

"At least that," Bernie said. "And more when they're wet. And even more when they're full of salmon. You'll see, Jake."

"Wow, sounds like a lot of heavy work."

Freddy laughed. "Got that right. An' to think we get to take 'em in every time we get a closure and set 'em out again with every opener. Think you're up to it?"

Jake gave Freddy's shoulder a squeeze. "Of course. I'm bigger than you."

It took a long time for the guys to set both nets. By the time they finished with the second one, Freddy took over the tiller. He swung the skiff around and headed back to the first net to start picking fish.

"Okay, Teacher," Jake said, winking at Freddy. "I'm still curious. How deep is the water here? Do the salmon swim high enough to go into the net? Or do they swim deeper so they miss the net? How do you know what to expect?"

Freddy pretended a deep sigh. "Don'tcha know nothin'? Guess I gotta remember this is your first time set-netting. Anyway, the deep end of the net sits in about sixty feet of water, which gets shallower towards shore. Reds swim high. In about the top five or six feet under the surface. Dogs, or chum salmon, swim deeper, maybe down ten feet, and the pinks somewheres between. You do know the difference between reds and dogs and pinks, dontcha?"

"I know that pinks are called humpies and dogs are chums. Do they mix with the reds when they swim towards the river to spawn?"

Freddy answered again as he kept steering the skiff towards the first net. "Takes practice to tell a red from a real bright dog. The pinks come through later in the summer. In big schools. Anyway, there's nothin' to worry about, Jake. Our nets'll miss some of the salmon going through, but we're sure to catch plenty. Your crew share will pay for another year of college … hopefully."

"How far away is the river where they spawn?"

"Bout twenty-five miles from here. The fish swim close to shore on their way over. That's why we can net so many," Freddy added.

Bernie told Jake that set-net fishing was a matter of laying a net wall in the water in the direct path of the fish. "Simple as that, Jake. And wait 'til you see some of those reds! They go as high as ten pounds. Like holding a bag of sugar. Most go around six pounds, though."

"Wow, I didn't realize set-net fishing was so complicated!" Jake said.

Once they reached the net, Bernie and Freddy started picking salmon out of the net where they'd been caught. Jake looked on. Freddy pointed to his uncle's two skiffs. "Pete 'n' Uncle Hal each take a skiff out alone. They think they can get more salmon by fishing separately. I think our way is better—all three of us workin' together. Not alone, like they fish."

*Sure hope Pete stays away. Don't want him ruinin' anything of Bernie's … or Jake's and mine, neither.*

"I see they're picking fish, too. From here, Pete doesn't look like such a menace, does he?" Jake closed his eyes, turning his head upward. "Time to send You a message, Lord. Please keep Pete away from us. You know my guts are churning just thinking about his bullying."

Freddy ignored Jake's prayer and thought about his own churning guts. With effort, he tore his thoughts away from his cousin and slowly cruised along the first net. But something out of the corner of his eye caught his attention. He glanced back towards Pete's skiff. Startled, he saw Pete raise his arm and hit a black object in the water. *What's he holding … a club? That's a seal he's hitting! No, Pete! Don't!*

Jake jerked around. "You okay, Freddy? Don't what? You look like you just saw a ghost."

Freddy swallowed hard. "Uh, n-nothin'." *If Pete's killin' seals, Uncle Hal could be in deep sh__ … trouble. Can't let Jake see Pete doin' it. Gotta talk to Pete. Do I dare? Or will he clobber me, too? What's he thinkin', anyway? Tryin' to ruin his dad's fishing business … his reputation? All the other camps know Uncle Hal's as honest and dependable as anyone.*

Bernie took over the tiller from Freddy and cruised alongside the net, keeping watch on the skiff's direction as he helped Freddy pick. Bernie gave Freddy a quick glance. "Hey, Teacher! Since you're so good at it, show Jake how to pick fish."

Freddy cleared his throat. "Yeah, you've been standin' there watchin' us long enough, Jake. Watch how I do this." He jerked a handful of net and picked a big, red salmon from one of its mesh holes.

Freddy swallowed, tried to concentrate. *Don't look towards Pete's skiff, Bernie! I can't have you see him killin' seals, neither. I know how touchy you can be sometimes. Besides, you already know Pete's trouble. What's Pete thinkin', anyway?How can he do this? And what can I do about it? Now I have another secret to keep. When will it end?*

Freddy tried to relax. "Your turn, Jake. Don't pop the fish out of the net. Pick it out like I'm doin'. Or … if it's stuck, cut it free. With your knife …." he pointed to the jackknife dangling from his float coat belt. "That way, only one strand of the net will break, and …."

"If you stretch the net and pop the fish out," Bernie interrupted with his mouth set, "you'll break the net apart. That's what we call a deckhand hole. I don't want any deckhand holes. Or bruised fish. Pick the fish out by pushing it through head first. Grab the gill behind its head and it should slide right through. If not, cut just one strand of the net. Only one. Got that?" For emphasis, he slapped the net against the side of the skiff.

"Sure, Boss," Jake said. "I won't pop 'em out."

Freddy watched Jake's hands as he worked. To start with, he was all thumbs. Every time Jake grimaced, Freddy knew Jake's hands were growing colder and sorer. He moved as slow as a snail. Freddy chuckled, remembering how slow *he'd* been the first time he picked fish. And how his shoulder and back muscles ached. He hoped Jake would be able to pick up the pace soon, or Bernie'd be on his case.

"Keep it up, Jake. It'll come." Freddy held up his pick—a small, metal hook. "Use your pick more. It'll help slide the net off the fish … like this." Freddy demonstrated the use of his metal pick.

They picked fish and picked some more. When they finished picking from the first net, they motored over to the second one. Even while wearing cotton gloves, it wasn't easy. Freddy had forgotten how slippery and heavy the fish could be. It took a lot of shaking to get some of them through the holes. The diamond-shaped mesh was the perfect size for hooking an unsuspecting salmon's gills good and tight.

Freddy stood up straight, rubbing his aching back. It hurt from constantly leaning over the side of the rocking skiff. The fish seemed to grow heavier and heavier. His nose burned from the sea salt he breathed in while bending over close to the splashing waves. Whitecaps hissed and danced on the water, noisier than the muffled sound of the trolling motor.

But they were catching fish! By the time the second net was empty, stinky fish flopped around and filled the bottom of the skiff nearly to the fishermen's knees.

"Time to haul these to the holding skiff, boys," Bernie said. "Pull up tight against it, Freddy, and tie the skiffs together … but don't scratch the paint!"

Freddy grinned. *Bernie and his new toy. He's as bad as a kid.*

When they reached the twenty-foot holding skiff, Bernie climbed in while Freddy carefully secured the two skiffs together. Bernie grabbed a brailer bag—a canvas-like, mesh bag that would hold about six hundred pounds of fish. "I'll hold the bag open," he said. "Jake, you and Freddy count each fish as you throw it in. Let's start with the pinks."

Bernie held the bag while the boys filled it with the humpies. He straddled the skiffs when the bag grew too heavy, resting it on the edge of the skiffs. "Hurry it up, boys, but don't lose count."

When the bag was filled, Bernie noted the count in a pocket-sized tablet he carried. "Let's get the chums out of the way, Freddy, then it's your turn to hold a bag for the reds. When it's filled, Jake can hold the next bag. Let's get this job done."

The bags held loops on each corner, meant to attach to a crane on the tender that would come by once or twice a day to pick up their fish. After they finished throwing, counting, and filling, Bernie placed a large, canvas cover over each brailer bag to keep the fish cool. He stood up straight, rubbing his lower back as he checked the count. He punched the air with his fist. "Three hundred eighteen reds, boys. Not bad for opening day! Let's hope we soon go above the average."

"What's the average?" Jake asked.

"About four hundred reds," Bernie said. "They average six pounds each. That's money, boys." He rubbed his hands together, a smile of glee stretching across his ruddy, usually solemn face.

The guys jumped back into the now-empty skiff and Bernie steered it through the choppy waves back to the first net. "Let's start in again, boys. Jake, you're doing a good job. Keep picking at the rate you've been and you'll soon be up to Freddy's speed."

Jake groaned. "Maybe, Boss. But how long before my back quits hurting?"

Freddy socked his shoulder. "Knew you couldn't take it."

"Yeah, you used to tell me that all the time on the *Danny Boy*," Jake countered.

Freddy laughed, punching the air with a victory sign. "You'll never hit my speed."

As they pulled up a portion of the net, Freddy was stunned to find a gaping, four-foot hole in it. He gulped. A glance at Jake's pale face showed he, too, had seen it. Freddy pursed his lips, knowing his lip scar had turned as vivid as a crimson crayon line.

*Chapter 5*

# A TORN NET

Bernie's face became a thunder cloud. "How did we miss that while picking this net? Were we in that big a hurry? I thought you boys mended both nets. Do I have to stay on your backs in everything you do?"

Freddy gasped. How dare Bernie blame them! His face burned with anger. He darted a quick glance at Jake, whose own face had turned as sun-bleached as a sea star beached at low tide. Huffing, he scowled at Bernie. But he didn't dare say anything. After all, he was on Bernie's payroll. He tucked his face into his coat collar, feeling sick.

"We couldn't have missed such a big hole, Bernie!" Jake yelled. "We went over every inch of both nets. But … how …?"

Bernie scowled at the boys. Jake stepped close to Freddy and whispered, "Were we too distracted by Pete's bullying when we were supposed to be mending, back there on the beach? Or when Joanie came down to see us? You have to admit, we *were* distracted." Jake turned to look Bernie in the eye. "It couldn't have been our fault. We went over those nets with eagle's eyes."

Bernie picked up the net to study the hole more closely. His face turned red with anger. "You boys missed this hole. See how it's been cut? Not jagged like the rest of the holes you mended. This is not a seal's work. It's Pete's work."

"No!" Freddy shouted. "He's mean, but he wouldn't cut your net." *Or would he? After all, I'd never have pictured him clubbing a seal, neither. I'm tired of defendin' the guy. Maybe I shouldn't any more. But … he'll tell everyone my secret if I rat on him. What about Uncle Hal, though? How bad will this hurt his fishin' business?*

Bernie's stare reeked of disbelief. It burned a hole in Freddy's gut. He knew his words didn't convince Bernie. With a shaky sigh, Freddy stared out towards Pete's skiff. *Somehow you'll pay for this, Pete. You wait 'n' see. Whatever happened to you? Used to be fun to be around when we were kids. Seems like after your mom died, you turned into a different person. Not one I like much, neither.*

Jake gave Freddy's arm a shake. "You know how he threatened me. Maybe it *was* your cousin. But why would he want to get back at me through Bernie?"

Freddy shucked off Jake's hand. Still staring out at sea, he saw a dark blob bouncing among the waves. He squinted hard. A slow smile stretched across his face as he pointed. "See that?" he yelled. "It's a Steller sea lion. They're death on nets. Coulda been him that did it." *Maybe it wasn't Pete after all. Or … was it? Guess I wouldn't put nothin' past him now. Who am I tryin' to kid?*

Bernie's skepticism couldn't be denied. He kicked at a dead salmon. "I guess it's possible the sea lion could have been the culprit. But ... could have been Pete, too." He shook his head as if to clear his thoughts. Raising a hand, he glared at both boys. "No time to fret and stew about it now. Let's finish picking this net and mend it later. It's too big a hole to mend out here. Especially in this choppy sea."

Jake grinned. Freddy faked a grin, too, but knew he couldn't hide behind it forever. *The Steller doesn't convince me. I still think it was Pete who done it. The cuts are too even. What am I s'posed to do? Just 'cuz Pete's blood, should I stick up for him? Even if he's doin' something illegal?*

The sea lion bobbed up and down in the waves. Jake pointed. "He looks like he's laughing at us. Freddy, you know all about marine mammals. Is that really a sea lion? I thought they were nocturnal. Is that true? Maybe that's a seal. What do you think?"

"Actually, sea lions aren't nocturnal," Freddy explained. "They're diurnal. And they love salmon. And they rip set-nets while grabbing the fish caught in the mesh." He looked hard at the bobbing animal. "It's a Steller, all right. It could've made them holes. Seals don't tear big holes like this. Seals are shy, and they nibble at the fish like finicky cats do. Guess it couldn't've been Pete's work."

*I still believe it was Pete's work. But I won't tell Jake that ... yet.*

Bernie snorted in disgust. "You're right, boys. Seals don't make big holes like this. They take little bites. But this torn net is a sea lion's work. They take the whole fish. Do lots of damage to nets. And that's what's swimming out there. Maybe it just doesn't know the difference between daylight and dark." He half-grinned, half-glared at Freddy and Jake, his half-attempt at a joke falling flat. "That's the end of it."

After an hour of tense, quiet picking, they finished the set and left the fish in the skiff. They'd dump and count at the holding skiff later. Once the net was free of fish, Bernie found the tear and cut a large panel from it, setting it aside. He and the boys mended the hole with a spare panel, threading the panel with mending line which Bernie always kept on hand in the skiff. Bernie mumbled to himself while they worked. Freddy knew he was frustrated about losing precious fishing time.

They headed for shore, Freddy scanning the shoreline. He smiled to himself, pleased to see Joanie walking down the hill with Jessica, who waddled behind her, stopping every few feet to inspect something on the path.

Once they reached shore, Bernie stopped short of the beach. "I'm leaving you here to mend this torn section, Freddy. It's too big a piece to waste. Jake and I will go out to pick the other net again. He needs the experience." Bernie handed Freddy the panel he had cut out to be mended.

Freddy stepped into the water, hoping against hope his boots were high enough to keep him dry as he stumbled through the surf.

"Ask Barb for the spool of mending twine and a needle," Bernie said. "She knows where it is."

They motored away. With his boots sloshing in water, Freddy reached the shore and began climbing the hill. When he met Joanie, he told her, "I'll be right back, Little Sis. Wait for me and we can take a walk." He ran to get the twine and needle, and hurried back down to the beach.

"What's up, Fred? You look stressed. And what's that squishing noise?" Joanie chuckled.

Ignoring her question, Freddy led the way north along the beach towards Hiding Rock, not ready to explain what happened. "Let's take a walk. I got time before I mend this torn net and they come back to pick me up."

Joanie nodded. She held Jessica's hand on the way to Hiding Rock where a small tidal pool shimmered in the sunlight near the rock. Jessica, squealing, wiggled free and squatted on the sand to touch a purple sea star. The beach at low tide was littered with them. The brilliant orange, red, yellow, green, and deep blue sea stars created a kaleidoscope of color.

Jessica pointed. "What's dat?"

"It's a frilled anemone. Ain't … isn't it pretty?" Freddy and Joanie studied its white tentacles that extended from a long, curly body.

"An' dat?" Jessica touched a plate limpet. She tried to pry it off the rock it shared with dozens more limpets. "Can't, Joanie. You."

Joanie laughed. "Sorry, Jess, it's stuck."

Freddy pried it off the rock and placed it into Jessica's outstretched hands. "See the muscles on its feet? Like suction cups. They won't let loose. These little guys usually come out at night and follow the tide water up and down the rocks."

Joanie whacked Freddy on the leg with her cane. "See? Told you! You're a born teacher."

Freddy grinned. "Come on. Follow me." He led the way inside Hiding Rock's miniature cave. The huge rock had a hole in it that curved into a hideaway. They had to stoop to enter.

Jessica again squealed with delight, this time at a wrinkly dogwinkle the tide had deposited on the cave floor. Its shell, covering the snail inside, was full of pretty ridges and frills.

"Ooh," Joanie said. "Spooky in here. Looks like a dark dollhouse."

"Don't ever let Jessica wander over here alone," Freddy warned. "Specially durin' flood tide. It comes in fast, you know. She could get trapped."

Joanie shrugged. "What do you take me for? Irresponsible? Of course, I won't."

"Jake's told me how scatterbrained you can be sometimes. Just consider it a warnin', Little Sis."

Joanie gave Freddy's arm a playful sock. "Your grammar's improving, Fred. You're a fast learner. Just watch those double negatives and dangling g's."

"Huh?"

"You know ... like 'Don't got no apples.' It means you have apples. Don't and no are both negatives. They cancel each other out. And be sure to say your g's. They're *hangin'* like dead fish on a hook."

Freddy laughed. "Okay, Teach. I got the message. But I'm curious. How did you get so smart? And don't your friends make fun of your perfect grammar?"

Joanie shrugged. "Guess I've always liked words. I love to read, and some of my friends are nerds, too." Blushing, she giggled.

"Just wonderin'. Don't mean to embarrass you."

On the way back to mend the net, Freddy told her about the cut net. "I think maybe Pete did it. So ... what do you think about him?"

She hesitated. "Well, he's kind of good looking in his own sort of way. But I can't deny he's a creep. He's pretty arrogant, and definitely a bully. You know, bullies usually act that way because they're trying to cover up something ... like being hurt by someone. Dad used to tell us not to judge others until we've walked in their shoes. I think Jake and I need to keep an open mind about Pete."

Freddy rubbed his prickly chin. "His mom died, you know. And Uncle Hal's a great guy, but he's too easy on Pete. Maybe that's it, huh?"

Joanie looked up at Freddy. "Could be. I just don't get why he'd want to cut a hole in Bernie's net, though, just to get back at my brother. Something's bothering him. Something maybe deeper than his mom's death. Something we don't know about ... or do *you* know something about your cousin?"

*Could it be about Mattie almost drowning?* Freddy wondered why Pete tormented him about that awful day.

He gave his head a mental shake as he worked on the torn net. A snicker and a grin spilled out of his lips. "Don't tell me you're good at the mental stuff, too?"

Joanie sighed. "I may be scatterbrained at times, but I do make sense. I've always been smart. So there. My dad's a chaplain, you know. Some of his 'mental stuff' learning has rubbed off on me, I guess."

Freddy chuckled. "You sure do blush easy, Little Sis." He gave her ponytail a playful tug. Laying the net aside, he picked up Jessica, adding, "Don't she, Jess? … Uh, doesn't she, Jess? And you're right. You are scatterbrained." He tossed the toddler in the air and caught her before tickling her until she giggled.

Blushing deeper, Joanie stuck her hands on her slender hips and stamped her foot. "You and Jake are just alike! Always thinking the worst. I don't think the worst about *you.*" Joanie's voice dropped to a whisper. "In fact, I'm thankful you help my brother. God has changed him since you guys were rescued last winter. And I think God used *you,* Fred, to do some of that changing. He talked a lot about you after the disaster at sea. He told me how you taught him everything about crab fishing and stuff … and how you risked your life saving the diary he wrote for me."

Still blushing, Joanie covered her whispered words with her hand. Her gaze locked his and instantly changed to a sparkling tease. She flipped her ponytail and with a teasing, sideways glance, added, "Even if your grammar is atrocious and you dress like a slob and your hair is a greasy mess, you're my … um, my hero. If you must know."

Freddy felt his own face heating up. Not used to such compliments—and teasing criticism—he stared at the beach. He didn't feel like a hero. Ever. But … recovering, he puffed up his chest. "'Course I'm a hero. You're right about that, Little Sis."

Joanie chuckled. "Nothing egotistical about you, is there?"

Freddy sighed dramatically as he picked up his mending needle again. "There you go with them big words again, Little Sis." Freddy thought about the weeks on the *Danny Boy* when he had teased Jake. At first angry because his cousin Pete had lost out on Jake's job, he began to see that Jake was so wet behind the ears he needed help. From then on, Freddy made sure Jake didn't get into trouble. He had to keep his new friend safe then, and he wanted to keep him safe now. Would that make him a hero?

"So … how about our deal, Fred?" Joanie, sitting next to him, held Jessica around the waist. "Your grammar for my art education. Remember? I'm helping you with your grammar. When do we start my education?"

Freddy looked up at her grinning face. "How about soon as I finish this net? We might have a few minutes if I hurry."

As Freddy finished, Jake yelled across the water from the skiff. Freddy laughed at Jake jumping up and down and yelling and throwing his arms straight out to the side. *Woohoo! Must mean they picked an extra big red with no bite marks on it. Yes! Maybe this time I'll make enough money so Mom can quit one of her jobs. I owe it to her. Maybe I can even put some away for college …. College? Me? Sure would love to teach little kids, though. Naw, I'd probably screw that up, too.* Freddy shook his head to banish such thoughts.

While waiting for the skiff, Freddy led Joanie towards the hillside cottonwood.

Joanie held Jessica's hand. "Look, Jess! A wild rose. Mm, it smells good."

Freddy helped Jessica hold one to her nose without thorns pricking her fingers.

"These are called prickly roses. The natives used to call them the Itchy Bottom plant." Freddy snickered. "Of all the roses, it's the only native one in Alaska. This bloom is out a little early this year. Guess the sun warmed the soil just right for it."

As they walked along, Freddy pointed to a cluster of white Pasque Flowers.

"They look like old men whose beards had a bad hair day," Joanie said with a quiet giggle."

Freddy guided Jessica's hand along the silky hairs of one flower. "Feels like a kitty, doesn't it, Jess?"

"Kitty soft. Me pick?"

"No, Jess." Joanie removed her hand. "God intended us to enjoy wildflowers in their natural state. Right, Fred?"

Freddy grunted. "You sure do talk like a grown-up, Little Sis. But … it's not against the law to pick 'em in Alaska." He thought about the times he had helped his sisters pick wildflower bouquets for their mom.

On their way back to the beach, Joanie stopped him with her hand. "Look, Fred. The land is bursting in yellows and purples and … and this is just the beginning. I can hardly wait for full summer color." She rubbed her hands together. "My fingers just itch to sketch and paint some of these flowers."

Freddy pointed to the buds of Common Fireweed and Alaska Cotton. "The Fireweeds are my favorites. Know why they're called Fireweed?"

Joanie snickered. "Anyone knows that, Fred. They're such bright shades of pink and purple, they look like fire."

"Wrong. The Fireweed is the first plant that grows back after a wildfire." Freddy grabbed hold of her cane and swung it against her leg. "And don't forget it!"

"Well … I do know that Fireweed honey and jam are delicious. We bought some at a gift shop once."

"Yeah, and you can eat the flowers and stems, too. We'll try it later in the summer … if you dare, that is."

Joanie sent a glaring look his way. "Of course I dare. Whenever you're ready."

While they waited on the beach, Joanie helped Jessica build a sand castle. She cleared her throat. "Uh, Jake doesn't know it yet, Fred, but our dad is sick."

"Oh? What's wrong with him?"

"I think it might be his heart. While Jake was in college last semester, Dad started having problems. Jake didn't see him for weeks at a time. Then, after his college finals, Jake drove us right to Homer where he left his car at our aunt's house before we caught the ferry to Kodiak. And here we are. Jake hasn't had a chance to notice Dad's health deteriorate."

Joanie looked into Freddy's eyes. "So what do you think, Fred? Our parents will be coming to visit soon. Should I tell Jake about Dad? Or wait and let him find out on his own?"

"Don'tcha think you should tell Jake now? Prepare him? Either way, he's going to worry."

Joanie sighed, stirring the sand with her cane for a long time. "No, I think I'll wait. No sense worrying him any longer than necessary."

"Yeah, maybe you're right." Freddy pictured his own mom lying in bed sick with cancer a couple years ago. Good thing the chemo did the trick and she was cured. Good thing, too, her treatments took place in winter when he could be at home to take care of his sisters and help his mom. Even if he did lose out on winter fishing. He remembered how grateful she had sounded for his help. But he knew she was still disappointed in him.

*If only I hadn't let her down with Mattie at the pool that day. She'll probably never forgive me. She's gone through so much. Bad enough Dad left us. Maybe that was my fault. Can I ever make it up to her?*

Freddy barely heard Joanie's words. "Uh, sorry, Little Sis. Guess I was day-dreamin' ... day-dreaming, I mean." He stood up. "The guys'll be here soon. Don't mind me, but I've gotta jog a little to stretch my legs some more. See you later."

Freddy took off at a run uphill towards the misshapen cottonwood. Overlooking the ocean and vulnerable to ocean winds, it leaned eastward, alone on Eagle Point. Every year a pair of eagles added to their huge, sprawling nest near the top and raised a new brood.

When he reached the old tree, he looked up at the nest wondering if it held eggs yet, and how many. He stood under the tree and looked around. Such a peaceful spot. He was glad he had brought Joanie and Jessica up here. Spring wildflowers of every color and kind surrounded him. Honey bees buzzed around emerging berry blossoms. The blossoms would grow to be gigantic just as the berries they'd produce. Sweet, yellow salmonberries, blueberries, black crowberries, cloud berries, all much bigger than the wild raspberries Jake talked about that grew in Wisconsin. In a few weeks Freddy and the others would be picking them for pies. He'd have to bring Joanie here again to sketch when they had more time.

He closed his eyes, inhaling the scent of flowers and soil and sea. But it wasn't enough to keep his thoughts from skittering back and forth. He kept picturing his dad, drunk and mean, and how he had tried to protect his mom and sisters from his dad's angry fists. He remembered how relieved he felt when his dad left. But drunken mean or not, he still wondered what happened to him.

Freddy's thoughts skittered over to Hal and Pete. *Jake sure looks like Pete, now that I think about it. Jake's lucky to have a dad. Sure hope nothing bad's wrong. But what if Uncle Hal is his real dad? That would be weird. What a shocker for Jake if he found out Pete might be his brother. Wow, that'd make Jake my cousin! Okay by me, but how would Jake feel?*

Freddy remembered Jake saying his real dad had died years ago. Maybe he didn't die after all. Maybe Hal really was his dad. No, Freddy thought, it couldn't be. It must be true that everyone does have a twin somewhere. Even if that did sound stupid. Maybe Freddy had a twin somewhere, too.

*The whole subject of dads freaks me out … reminds me of the soaps Ma watches on TV.*

Pulling his thoughts away from soap opera scenarios, Freddy vowed at least to keep Jake's spirits up. He jogged a while before starting back downhill. A big flock of kittiwakes flew off in a mad rush. Not far away, a red fox scampered off too, like something chasing it. Then Freddy heard it. He whirled around and his breath caught.

## *Chapter 6*

# KODIAK!

A huge Kodiak bear stood only twenty feet away. One ragged ear stuck out like a black eye. Freddy froze. His heart stopped. His brain felt on fire. Fast as lightning, Freddy's gaze ran back and forth in an arc from the bear to Sitting Rock. Was the bear downwind? Had it seen Freddy? Or would it walk away, intent on something else? Freddy held his breath as the giant bear dropped to all fours and lumbered past, taking its own sweet time.

Sweat poured down Freddy's face, his neck, his back. Step by slow, backward step, he made his way downhill. Joanie and Jessica! They had to be okay. Intent on not tripping and alerting the brown bear, Freddy finally reached Sitting Rock where the two girls played in the sand, unaware. He looked back uphill and glimpsed the bear galloping away. He let out his breath in a gush.

Joanie squinted up at him. "What's wrong?" She stood up.

Freddy pointed. "A bear. I'm walking you and Jess back to the cabin. Gotta hurry, though. Come on."

"Why? I'm not scared of a little black bear, Fred. I'm not a wimp." She pulled away when he took hold of her arm.

"I'm tellin' you, it weren't no little black bear. There ain't no black bears on Kodiak. Your mind is back in Wisconsin. It was a huge Kodiak. You comin'?"

Joanie sighed, scowling. "Okay, okay. Let's go back … and Fred, you're reverting to your old habits of grammar."

Freddy gritted his teeth. "Ain't you afraid of nothin'?" He grabbed Jessica and led the way uphill, trying to hurry Joanie along. Once inside the cabin, he plunked Jessica in front of Barb. "You gotta call Fish and Game. Now. There's a brown bear out there.

Joanie, standing in the doorway, stomped her feet. "Does this mean I can't go out and sketch anymore?"

"Not today, that's for sure," Freddy said.

"Can't they catch the bear and move it? I can't stay inside all day! Neither can Jessica."

"They're not allowed to move bears. Don't take chances, Little Sis. I'm serious. It ain't worth it. Besides, Jake would have our hides if he knew you were bear bait."

Barb grabbed the CB radio to report the bear sighting. "Here, Freddy," she said, handing him the speaker. "You talk. You know more about it."

After Freddy described the where and what and when, he asked the ranger, "Anybody else seen a brown bear around? I'm sure it was a boar. About nine hundred pounds, I'd guess."

A static-filled voice responded. "Yeah, a couple other guys reported one earlier. Over by the slough. We'll keep an eye out and let the other camps know, too. I doubt it'll hang around for long, though. Not to worry."

Freddy thanked the woman on the line, exhaling a sigh of relief. He knew all the neighboring camps would already know about it, since they were all on the same party line. Most of the fish camps kept their CBs on day and night. Like a household of family members, Freddy thought, there could be no secrets. Guess that was a good thing, considering.

"Gotta go. They're waitin' … waiting for me at the beach." He ran out the door and down to Bernie and Jake who waited in the skiff.

"Where have you been, Freddy?" Bernie's eyes blazed, his voice harsh and demanding.

Freddy picked up the panel of newly-mended net, waded into the surf, and flung it into the boat. "Been trying to get away from a brown bear, that's where." He climbed in, glad Bernie would be handling the tiller for a while. He needed time to calm down.

Jake grinned at him. "A Kodiak? Seriously? Wish I had seen him."

"No, you don't. He was huge. I walked Joanie and Jessica back to the cabin. Wasn't taking any chances. That's why I'm late."

Bernie frowned. "Hmm. Better radio Fish and Game again."

"Barb and I already did. They said they'd 'keep an eye on it.' Those were their exact words. Said a couple others saw it, too."

"Keep an eye on it, huh? Sure wish they weren't so dead set against moving the devils. I guess that means you guys'll be wanting to sleep in the cabin tonight. Right?" Bernie grinned.

"I ain't … I'm not scared, if that's what you mean, Boss." Freddy thumped his chest.

"Yeah, right." Jake punched his arm. "Easy for you to say in this safe skiff. Besides, wasn't it you who woke me up last night? You thought you heard a bear, remember?"

Freddy grinned. "Well, let's hope it leaves the area so we won't have to be on guard every minute."

As they motored out to a set-net, Freddy groaned at the thought of more hard work ahead. His legs still felt as limp as fishing line. He hoped they wouldn't find any more holes in the nets. But no use worrying.

The warm air cheered his spirits. So did the big catch of salmon. After two pickings, the holding skiff rode low on the water from the weight of nearly two tons of fish. No new tears in the nets, but some of the red salmon had small bites taken out of them.

"Are these seal bites?" Jake asked as they sorted the salmon.

"Yep. The seals see a fish in the net and find it an easy meal. The salmon are too damaged to sell, so we'll have them for dinner tonight." Freddy counted lots of them. He shook his head and groaned. "We can't make money this way."

"Don't worry," Bernie said. "It may look like a lot, but the percentage is usually quite low. Not like last year. Remember, Freddy? We hardly had a decent meal of salmon, there were so few damaged. It's one of the downsides of set-netting for salmon. No use getting shook up about it. "

Freddy kept working, growing more tired by the minute. He glanced over to Jake, who was dragging his butt. "Hey, Jake! Remember on the *Danny Boy* when I said you couldn't take it? Looks like it's the same old story."

Jake chuckled. "You won't see me giving up. I didn't then, either. Remember? I stuck it out no matter how tired I got."

"Yeah, I gotta admit, you were a trooper." As they worked, Freddy couldn't help grinning. Jake had turned out to be a great friend.

Jake smiled in return. Clearing his throat, he said in a husky voice, "I thank God for you, Freddy. In spite of your teasing and tormenting, you helped me through that tough rescue."

Freddy's face warmed. In fact, his whole insides warmed, and not from the sun. But he wondered if Jake would still be smiling when he learned about his dad's illness.

The three fishermen kept picking fish, transferring and counting them until the tender came to relieve their heavy-laden holding skiff.

The tender operator steered his eighty-foot trawler next to their holding skiff. "Looks like you've got a good start, Bernie."

With quick precision, the men hauled Bernie's brailer bags into their boat, weighed them, and recorded the results on a receipt. Handing a copy to Bernie, the skipper said, "See you soon, guys. We'll let you know when. Keep up the good work."

Bernie tossed the lines and maneuvered the skiff away from the huge tender.

The next time around, another tender would come. Two of them rotated, one picking up brailer bags from set-netters like Bernie, the other making a twelve-hour run to the cannery at the city of Kodiak waterfront. They also made necessary grocery runs for the various fish camps.

Bernie's smile could have reached the Bering Sea. "Good work, guys. A great start to the season. Let's hope it continues. Now let's get back to work."

Would the day ever end? Freddy's shoulders ached and so did his lower back. His feet tingled with cold in spite of the warm afternoon. He knew Jake felt the same tiredness, but without the misery of having cold, wet feet from sloshing through the surf earlier. Listening hard to Jake's muttered words, he heard him pray, "Lord, give me the same energy You gave me on the *Danny Boy* when we faced those williwaws."

Jake's words alone infused Freddy with a surprising burst of energy. Without thinking, he, too, muttered a word of thanks heavenward.

Before quitting for the day, Bernie used a power hose on board to clean the nets.

"Would you look at that algae and junk!" Jake shouted. "And all the jelly fish stuck to the nets."

Freddy held up a portion of a net for Bernie to hose down. "Yeah, and those buggers don't help the nets any, either, with all the slime they leave."

Jake tapped Freddy on the side of his head. "Hey, your grammar's improving already. Good job."

"Yeah, well, your little sis won't let up on me."

At ten o'clock the crew headed for the cabin. After a late but tasty dinner, Freddy and Jake turned down Joanie's request for a game of Monopoly. Instead, they dashed into their tent to bring in their sleeping bags. They sacked out near the door of the cabin. Soon Bernie and the others went to bed, too.

In the quiet, Jake leaned over, pulling Freddy's big toe that stuck out from his sleeping bag. "I hope you didn't leave any food in the tent. Sure don't want to have it ruined in case another bear comes around. Or maybe the same bear."

Freddy groaned and slapped Jake's hand away before sleep stole any further thoughts.

The next day was a replica of the day before. The crew picked and hauled fish, rushed through lunch, and picked and hauled some more. Freddy hardly had time to think about confronting Pete about the torn net … and the seal he killed. He hadn't even seen his cousin.

While picking salmon that afternoon, they heard a helicopter overhead. Bernie killed the motor of his skiff so they could watch the chopper fly back and forth behind the hill where their cabin stood. The chopper hovered low over one spot for some time before it lifted off and flew in a wide sweep away from them towards the city of Kodiak. Freddy hoped its noisy rotor scared the bear away for good.

As the crew continued to fish, Freddy reveled in the calm seas, such a welcome change from yesterday's rough chop. Ripples of water like frothy meringue danced all around the skiff. The ripples sizzled as a pod of porpoises circled their boat.

Jake leaned over to watch them. "Hey, guys! Looking for a free handout?" He smiled and returned to picking fish. "Look at 'em dance. You can almost hear them laugh."

Freddy smiled as the porpoises cavorted among the ripples. The pleasant sight helped lighten his task.

At the sound of a motor off a ways, Freddy squinted into the sun. It was Pete! He stood in his skiff, shouting at something in the water. Freddy watched in shock as Pete lifted his wicked club and whacked hard at something over and over. Pete's angry shouts punctuated the sea air. Freddy hoped Jake and Bernie didn't hear.

*The murderer! What's wrong with Pete? Killing another seal. He won't get away with this. But how am I gonna keep anyone else from finding out so it doesn't ruin things for Uncle Hal? Fish camp has been his life. And how long can I keep Pete from ratting on me about my secret?* Freddy wondered where Hal was. Maybe in the cabin, he thought. He coughed and gagged to cover the sound of Pete's murderous deed.

"You okay, Freddy?" Bernie asked. "Not catching a cold, are you?"

"Naw, just swallowed wrong is all." Freddy kept working and coughing through his lie.

Jake shaded his eyes, peering out at the ocean. "Well, I heard someone shout. Didn't you, Freddy?"

"Yeah, just Pete acting up. See him out there showing off? Probably caught an extra big red and wanted his dad to know."

Jake shrugged, returning to his work. Freddy let out his breath. *That was close.*

Later that day, Freddy's heart stopped at the sight of a bloated seal floating on the water right ahead of the bow. Puncture wounds dotted its side and purple bruises surrounded each wound. Freddy's stomach heaved until he gagged. This time he wasn't faking it.

"What the ...?" Bernie swore as he leaned over to have a look. "Looks like this seal's been beaten! No mammal I know would leave marks like this." His eyes narrowed. "Unless it's the two-legged kind. This doesn't add up."

He turned to stare at Freddy. "You know anything about this?" Bernie spat out his words.

Freddy spread out his shaking hands. "Hey, Boss, don't come down on me! I didn't do it. Didn't have a thing to do with it." *I feel like killing Pete. Cousin or not. Bully or not. Threatening me or not. And I'm sick of lyin' through my teeth to Bernie.*

Freddy could have sworn and cried at the same time. He knew that the Marine Mammal Protection Act prohibited the taking of all sea mammals. He knew that meant no harassing or killing of them. He knew what Pete had done was clearly illegal, not to mention cruel. And somehow he'd make him pay—when he got his courage up—so Uncle Hal wouldn't have to.

A tense silence finished the rest of their sixteen-hour day of picking fish. During supper, however, Jessica's antics brought a relaxed atmosphere to the fishermen. So did Bernie's later announcement.

"Jake, your parents are flying in tomorrow. You and Freddy take the skiff to meet them at the village airstrip in Akhiok. I'll have Barb pick fish with me while you're gone. Joanie can watch Jessica."

Jake flung both arms in the air and nearly tipped backwards in his chair. "Yes! Joanie, I can hardly wait."

"How did you find out, Bernie?" Joanie asked. "I thought they weren't coming until late next week."

"Guess you were outside with Jess when Barb took the call. I decided not to tell you until now. Thought maybe Jake would be good for nothing on the job." Bernie's lips turned up in a smile.

Jake whooped. "Guess that means I'd better clean up before we leave for Akhiok, huh?"

Freddy grimaced. "I'll say. You stink!"

"Oh, yeah? So do you. I'll beat you to the shower, Freddy." Jake shot out the door like a bullet.

"Just don't go using all the hot water, or you'll be sorry," Freddy yelled.

Their showers would have to be short. Water for household use came from a nearby creek which Bernie had piped into the cabin years ago. He had even constructed a private, outside shower stall. Jake filled a galvanized container with water, heated it on the stove, and carried it up a ladder where he dumped it into the shower tank. Soon Freddy heard him whistling a fast tune while enjoying his quick shower.

Jake came out dressed in clean jeans, his dark hair dripping. "Okay, Freddy, your turn. And by the way, did you clean out your side of the tent yet? It reeks."

Freddy mumbled to himself but took his much-needed shower. That night in their tent, clean and tired, he didn't even think about bears.

The next morning, Jake bounced around like a kid on a pogo stick.

Freddy laughed. "Hey, I know you're excited, but aren't you overdoing it?"

He and Freddy dressed for their trip to Ahkiok, ate breakfast, and headed down the hill to the skiff with Bernie in the lead.

Bernie stopped short. "What the ….?"

The empty skiff rocked in the waves a hundred yards away, heading out with an ebb tide.

*Chapter 7*

# BOAT ADRIFT

Freddy checked the line that always secured it to its mooring each night. It had been cut through. He knew Pete had set their skiff adrift.

"Freddy!" Bernie yelled. "Run over and get your uncle Hal. Hurry."

Freddy sprinted next door. In minutes, Hal was racing to his own skiff. He soon towed theirs to shore where Jake and Bernie pulled it up onto the sand. Once Bernie tied both ends of the line together so the skiff would be secure, they all huddled around the broken ends, inspecting them, trying to guess what caused the break.

As Freddy checked the line, Jake gasped and stepped back, ducking his head.

Freddy realized this was the first time Jake had seen Hal up close. Freddy's gaze darted from Jake to Uncle Hal and back. *They sure do resemble each other.*

When Jake appeared ready to bolt, Freddy laid a hand on his arm. "Steady. It'll be okay," he whispered.

A ragged sigh slipped through Jake's quivering lips. Freddy could almost hear his friend's heart thumping double time. *Poor kid. He's scared spitless.* He released his hold on Jake, who walked over to the skiff, head bent.

Hal, his gaze still on the line and obviously unaware of Jake's reaction, interrupted Freddy's thoughts. "Maybe it was a bear."

Bernie cackled. "No way, Hal. See any bear tracks around?"

"They could have been washed clear by the tide," Hal's lame voice added.

Bernie slammed a fist into his open hand. "You're in denial! Can't you see the line was cut?"

Freddy cringed. *Oh, God. Please don't let them come to blows. They've been friends for too long.*

Hal set his lips in a tight line. "I'll go get Pete. He's eating breakfast." His shoulders slumped as he headed to his cabin.

Freddy walked over towards Jake. *Hal knows Pete did it. What does Jake think? Or is he too upset about seeing Hal for the first time? Who's right about this? Was it Pete's dirty work? Or did an accident cause it?*

Freddy felt sorry for his uncle who was dragging his son towards the others. He didn't feel sorry for Pete, though. Freddy watched him try to jerk away from his dad's hard grip.

"Let me go … I didn't do it!" Pete shouted. "You gotta believe me!"

Hal's blotched face moved nose to nose towards Pete. "You better be telling the truth, Son. Or you'll have hell to pay." Another yank to Pete's arm sent him sprawling on the sand.

"I didn't do it, Dad! I didn't!" He stumbled to his feet, whimpering.

Hal stomped back to their cabin as Pete turned towards his skiff, stepping around everyone else. Freddy hissed, "You're gonna pay for this, Pete. I'll see to it."

"You better believe it, Pete," Bernie said, his voice tight and hard as he untied his skiff. "But we're running behind. You boys take me out to the holding skiff and then get moving towards Akhiok. Jake, your parents will be waiting."

Bernie climbed into the skiff and looked hard at Pete's retreating back. "We'll get to the bottom of this yet, Pete."

Freddy and Jake shoved the skiff out and jumped in, Freddy taking the tiller. After they dropped Bernie off at the holding skiff, he said, "Go ahead, boys. I'll go in for Barb and we'll pick salmon together until you get back."

Freddy headed south against a southwest wind that brought a sharp bounce to the skiff. Jake sat at the bow to give it extra weight while Freddy guided it. Sea spray brought a sting to Freddy's eyes and face.

"How far is it?" Jake shouted, shifting his body to face Freddy.

"About half an hour." *Jake looks more like he lost his best friend than he does eager to meet his parents.* Trying to lighten the mood, Freddy swerved the skiff from side to side until Jake lost his balance. But Jake didn't laugh. Freddy tried another tactic. "Look over there to the west, Jake. You'll see right about the place our boat went down."

They both studied the whitecaps coming at them in steady lines and the long rollers moving from southwest to northeast across the Alaska peninsula. Freddy envisioned Portage Bay straight across. After six months, he still had vivid thoughts about the loss of their boat and the terrible struggle to survive. He tried switching mind-gears to something pleasant. Like Jake seeing his mom and dad again. But maybe that wouldn't be so pleasant, either, because soon Jake would be able to tell if his dad was really sick. They'd both find out in a hurry if Joanie's statement about his illness had been right.

The ride to Akhiok was not only rough, it started to drizzle. Freddy hoped the Bergrens would be smart enough to wear raingear. As he motored around the south tip of land towards Akhiok, he pulled his wool cap over his ears and tucked his head into his warm collar.

At the dock near the airstrip that ran along the shore of the small, native village, Freddy hopped out of the skiff and tied the line to a piling at the tiny pier. Jake's parents sat hunched over and dripping wet on a big rock next to the nearby airstrip.

Jake's mom rushed over to him, arms outstretched. "Jake. You've grown an inch since I saw you last!" She swept him into a long hug.

He laughed. "Sure, Mom. How long has it been? Two weeks?"

His mom chuckled. "You know what I mean."

"Hey, Mom! You're shorter than I am now. In two weeks!" Jake laughed.

She placed her hands on his shoulders. "Looks like the Lord's been good to you, Son."

"Oh, yeah? How's that, Mom?"

"Well, you're … you're healthy looking. And bulkier. And … and beefier."

Freddy's laughter erupted like an Alaska volcano. He remembered calling Jake "Beef" after their sea rescue.

"Where's the plane?" Jake asked as he leaned into his dad's generous hug.

Mr. Bergren grimaced. "The pilot was in a hurry to get back to town. A fog bank coming in, he said. So he literally dropped us off and left. We're grateful when he threw our luggage out, it ended up in one piece." His grimace changed into a wide smile.

"Yeah, that's life on Kodiak Island," Jake said. "But you're here now and that's what counts." He turned to Freddy. "Hey, Freddy, you remember my dad. Freddy was my sidekick on the *Danny Boy*, remember, Dad?"

Freddy, polite and somber, shook hands with Jake's dad and then his mom. "Glad to see you again, Mr. and Mrs. B. Um, Jake ... we can't waste time. That front is moving in here, too."

Freddy helped settle Jake's parents at the center of the skiff on a wooden box Bernie had put down for them. Relieved they wore raingear, he made sure they sat protected from the wind. Seated at the bow as Jake steered, Freddy faced Jake's parents. He wanted to study Mr. B, to see if he really was sick as Joanie had said.

Between the motor roar and the wind, none of them could hear each other speak so they gave up trying to converse. Unsurprisingly, Mrs. B's face lost color with each curling wave they traveled up and over. Jake's dad's face was pale, too, but more gray than white. *Joanie's probably right about their dad being sick.* Freddy caught Mr. B reaching into his jacket pocket for a tiny pill or something he placed under his tongue.

Jake must have seen him dig in his pocket, too. "What are you doing, Dad?" he shouted, pointing to the object.

Mr. Bergren shrugged, as if to say it was nothing. Freddy didn't believe him. Would Jake?

Freddy could see that Jake's mom was miserable. Jake had told him that back in Wisconsin, where she grew up, she didn't even enjoy being out on small lakes—let alone Lake Superior, where her family fished regularly.

As Jake guided the tiller with one hand, Freddy studied him and his mom closely. He could see a slight resemblance. The likeness of his uncle Hal was much more pronounced. *The way Jake's jaw is set, he must be wonderin' who his real dad is. He must feel like a throw-away clam. I feel sorry for him. Wish I were a mouse in his mind right now. He looked mighty shook up when he saw Hal this morning. If Uncle Hal's Jake's real dad, that'll open up a can of worms.*

Freddy's concentration returned full-bore when he turned and saw a stone-wall fog bank drifting towards them. They'd have to hurry to beat the fog. He could already smell its thick brine, feel its clamminess right through his heavy rain gear. No doubt Jake's folks could feel it even more.

Jake steered at full throttle through the waves and wind and rain. Freddy could tell by the set of Jake's jaw that he had nothing in mind now except the weather. That was how things were in Alaska. Everything depended on the weather. They'd better be paying close attention.

Jake let up on the throttle as they finally neared Eagle Point fish camp. Not far out, in the deepening mist, Bernie and Barb were heading back from picking fish. They waved and hollered in answer to Jake's shouts. By the time both skiffs reached the beach, Freddy could barely see the cabin.

Jake pulled up onto the sand and Freddy helped the Bergrens out of the skiff. Above them, Joanie shouted a welcome through the fog as Jake secured the skiff to its mooring rock. Everyone hurried to the dry cabin. Jake's mom, although still pale from the ride, helped her husband up the hill. Freddy held Mr. B's free arm for added support. *His face looks like ash. His heart must be pumping like an oil well. Jake needs to get to the bottom of things. Fast.*

*Chapter 8*

# A MEETING

Inside, once warm and dry, everyone talked at once. Freddy crossed his arms and stood near the door to watch.

Mrs. B couldn't hug Joanie enough. "How's the babysitting?" she asked. "Are you minding your manners and paying attention?"

Mr. B sat on a chair taking it all in. Quiet, pale but smiling, he winked at Freddy.

When Bernie and Barb tromped in a few minutes later, a new round of introductions and welcomes took place. Barb hurried to set out food for lunch as Joanie watched Jessica. It would be crowded around the table at mealtime. Freddy wondered where the Bergrens would sleep during their visit.

Bernie must have read his mind. "Mr. and Mrs. Bergren, you can put your things on our bunk. Barb and I will sleep on the couch. It's a pullout."

Jake's mom protested. "Oh, but … we can't take your bed. And please call us Wendall and Sarah."

"If you'll call us Bernie and Barb. And about the beds, this isn't negotiable. You'll use our double bunk." Bernie looked stern, but Freddy saw through his wicked wink.

Hungry and tired by now, Freddy yawned. That got everyone's attention. They all laughed.

"Time to eat." Barb pointed out where everyone should sit at the table. They crowded around it, Freddy and Jake sitting on a makeshift bench Bernie had brought inside from behind the cabin.

After a short but emotion-packed prayer from Mr. B, they dug in, chattering away. Just as they finished eating, there was a quiet knock at the door.

At Bernie's invitation, Hal entered the cabin, holding his cap in one hand. "I just wanted to say ...."

Mrs. B gasped, covered her face with a napkin, and ran from the table where she had sat next to Freddy. She tripped on the table leg as she hurried towards the back door. "H-have to go t-to the outhouse," she whispered. Like a cornered puppy let loose, she bolted through the door, slamming it behind her.

Freddy glanced around at everyone else. They all looked as puzzled as he felt, especially Hal. Jake, meeting Freddy's gaze, shrugged his shoulders. But his pallor and frown told Freddy a different story.

"What's going on?" Jake asked, his voice raspy.

Hal shifted his feet, worrying his cap between his hands. "Um, I hope there's nothing wrong. I just came to tell you that the DNR radioed me earlier. There's another nuisance bear hanging around. Three other camps reported it. An old sow, traveling alone ... well, guess I'll be going." He pivoted and started to walk out the front door when Sarah charged back inside.

Pointing to Hal with a shaking finger, she demanded, "Are you ... H-hal?"

Everyone sat, stunned, until Bernie got up and grabbed Jessica in one quick swoop. He jerked his head for Barb to follow. "Looks like something personal going on. We'll see you later. You need to sort this out." He pulled three rain jackets free from their hooks by the door. "You coming too, Freddy?"

"In a minute."

Bernie slammed the door shut so hard, everyone jumped. Hal choked on a laugh that was thick with tension. Sarah dropped into a chair. Her hands became tangled knots in her lap, her breath coming quick and hard. Joanie and Jake stood behind her, as if to keep her from collapsing in a sobbing heap.

While Freddy waited, Sarah lifted her head, gulping air. "I-I thought you were dead! All these years ... I thought you were dead."

Her gaze pierced Hal as he stared at her, as visibly shaken as she. "S-sit down, Hal. I have to know what happened. Jake has to know."

Hal sat on the edge of a chair opposite hers. He chewed on his lips, twirled his cap between his hands. "Why would you think that? I don't understand. Who told you I died?"

Surprise spread over her face. "Why, your mother told me. She wrote me a letter and sent it to …."

The door banged open. "Freddy!" Bernie yelled. "Get out here!"

*I'd give anything to stay and hear this drama play out.* Freddy sighed, deciding he'd better leave. But once outside, his steps lagged. Not fifty feet from the cabin, he hunkered down on the trail, hunched over but with ears tuned to the shouts and crying that went on behind the closed door.

Freddy discovered that the door hadn't latched, however, and the family's shouts and cries followed him. Relieved to see Bernie and Barb chasing Jessica nearer the shore, Freddy listened intently. Between the wind blowing and his boss's playful shouting, he caught only snatches of the heated conversation.

Jake's shouts: "… all this time I could have … why wasn't I told?"

Hal's explanation: " … married … came home drunk … celebration … shoved her … don't remember … divorce papers."

Mrs. B's shrill, tear-filled apology: "Jake … so sorry … shock to me too … back to Wisconsin where I … happened so fast."

The door slammed shut. Freddy jerked his head around when, not five seconds later, the door opened. Jake's tearful yell tore at Freddy's heart. "No! Let me go … I'm out of here!"

## *Chapter 9*

# DEALING WITH IT

Jake ran down the hill, nearly colliding with Freddy. He tripped, rolled downhill until a boulder stopped him.

Freddy raced down to him. "Let me help." He gently wrapped his arms around Jake's chest to lift him but Jake jerked away.

"Leave me alone!" Sobbing, Jake headed to the cottonwood.

Freddy grimaced, knowing he'd have to wait to hear Jake's story. And to help him deal with it. He was convinced Jake had just learned Hal was his biological father.

His gaze followed Jake's erratic journey to the hillside tree until he caught a glimpse of Pete heading right for Jake.

*Uh-oh. Now what?* He winced as Pete gave Jake a hard shove. Waiting for the inevitable fight, Freddy was shocked to see Jake hold up his arms in defeat and walk on.

Pete headed towards Bernie's cabin. On the way, he stopped where Freddy sat on the ground. "What's up, Cuz? Where is everybody? And what's with all the shouting up there?" He looked up at the cabin.

"You'll find out soon enough," Freddy mumbled.

Pete toed Freddy in the back. "Tell me."

Freddy jumped up. "I said you'll find out soon enough." He sprinted towards the cottonwood.

*Oh, boy. Big trouble ahead. But … why should Jake have to deal with it alone? Somebody's gotta watch out for the poor kid. It's news enough to make a person wanna … no. I'm gonna help. Some way. If nothin' else, I'll follow him around. Make sure he doesn't do anything drastic.*

As Freddy ran, he couldn't help but know that Pete would make big trouble for Jake. The poor kid needed his protection more than ever.

Huffing hard, Freddy reached Jake and sat down on the wet grass. When Jake uncovered his face and turned, Freddy was not surprised to see how dazed he looked.

*Maybe I can cheer him up some.* "Hey, man, I'm here for you … an' remember, you're my cousin now—if I heard right. Blood cousins … how about that, huh? Think of all the stuff we can do together … go fishin' an' campin' an' …."

"Oh, shut up, Freddy! So what? I'm losing my dad! Losing him for somebody I don't even know. Losing Joanie as my sister. And … of all people, Pete's now my half-brother. It's enough to kill me! I hate …."

Jake looked towards the sea. "Tide's going out. Fighting with the incoming waves. That's just how I feel. Running against the tide. I hate this feeling. I hate …" Jake choked on his words.

Freddy could imagine somewhat how Jake felt. Sometimes he felt like hating his dad for leaving, and lately he hated Pete for all his dirty dealings. When he thought hard about it, he decided he hated himself more than anyone.

A bird flew overhead, singing a cheery song. Freddy looked up. Wispy clouds drifted along like the ocean tide on a calm day. The blue behind the clouds was so intense, he squinted and couldn't help but think how the beauty of the scene collided with the intensity of Jake's suffering.

"Wanna talk about it?" Freddy asked, hesitating to intrude too much, too soon.

Jake rose, nodded, and said, "Let's walk." He led the way slowly downhill to Sitting Rock, but before reaching the rock, Freddy jolted around when he heard footsteps behind them.

*Uh-oh. Not again. Pete heard the news. If he looks as mad as he's walkin', there's big trouble ahead.* "Jake! Watch out!" Freddy pushed him out of Pete's way but it was too late. With his heart in his throat, he almost felt the vibrations of Pete's killer punch that had Jake tumbling towards the water. Freddy fought Pete off Jake by throwing himself on top of him. He caught the brunt of Pete's vicious kick to his face. In agony, he reached for a handful of Pete's hair, pulling him down. As Pete's head jerked back, Freddy was shocked at the look of pure hatred on his face. Freddy's fear brought a shudder but he held on with a strength he knew only God could give. He slammed Pete to the ground and sat on his back.

"Get off me! I'm gonna kill him! He's no brother of mine … ever! Not ever!" Pete's words ended in a pathetic moan.

Freddy knew Pete's kick had broken his nose. He shuddered as he wiped the blood onto his T-shirt. A groan slipped past his swollen lips when he heard Joanie's cane plunk-plunking on the ground before he saw her. "Stay away, Little Sis," he managed. "You don't wanna get hurt."

But Joanie quickly backed up when she saw his battered face. "Dad! Come quick! Freddy's hurt." She screamed over and over until Bernie and Hal came running downhill.

"I'll take Pete from here, Freddy. And … thanks." Hal grabbed Pete's arm, forcing him up. He pulled him back to their cabin, Pete fighting all the way.

Freddy let Jake and Bernie help him to the cabin where Joanie and Mrs. B cleaned the blood off his face. When his nose stopped bleeding, they tended to his swollen lips and eyes. His pounding heart finally quieted and he tried thanking them for their efforts. But he felt limp as seaweed, succumbing to sleep.

When he awoke, Joanie stood over him, hands on hips, eyes twinkling as she scolded him. "Now you've done it, Fred. How are you going to teach me about the flora and fauna with your eyes half-shut?" She turned around to face her father who stood behind her. "Right, Dad?"

Freddy managed a guttural chuckle around his pain but knew a retort was useless. He didn't miss the look of utter sympathy on Mr. B's face.

After drifting off again, Freddy felt a light touch on his arm. Jake sat on a chair next to him. "Thanks, buddy. That kick was meant for me. I owe you one."

## *Chapter 10*

# HIDING ROCK

When Freddy awoke again, Jake told him that Barb went out fishing with Bernie again, so he and Freddy had the rest of the day off. "But he said to be sure and tell you that tomorrow we'll get no slack."

Freddy managed a grin. "I'll be ready."

Jake and Joanie both laughed. "You sound like you've got a mouthful of mud," Joanie said. "At least you don't need stitches. You'll heal, with the Lord's help."

By late afternoon, Freddy felt strong enough to get up. "Anyone up for a walk?" he asked.

Jake shook his head. "I'm gonna use this precious time off to visit with my mom and … um, dad. Joanie, why don't you and Jessica go?"

Freddy had hoped Jake would have joined him so he could learn what happened at the cabin earlier, but he said nothing.

Once outside, Freddy and Joanie picked their way slowly downhill while Jessica chattered, playing with the stones and shells she found. At Sitting Rock, Freddy spread his jacket across its dampness before he and Joanie sat down.

"No grammar lesson today, Freddy. I'll give your mouth a rest." She smirked.

He nudged her arm playfully. "You kiddin'? You mean I get the day off? Seriously, I guess all our brains are fried by now … what with your mom and Hal's upset. Wow! I didn't hear much, but caught enough to make me wonder why Jake and Pete are so mad. Just didn't expect Pete to be as mad as he was, though."

"Nor did I. I-I still don't know what to think. It sure puts a new spin on our whole family thing. I can imagine how my parents feel. And Hal. And … and *you*, Fred. How do *you* feel about it?" Joanie turned to look into his eyes.

Freddy cleared his throat. "Guess I need to hear the whole story first. I hate to see Jake so worked up. But I'm glad he's my new cousin … that is right, isn't it?"

Joanie nodded, stirring the sand with her cane and then grinning. "So much for giving your mouth a rest, Fred. Haven't heard you talk so much since … yesterday!"

Freddy grinned back. "But about Jake bein' my cousin. Sure beats having only Pete for a cousin. He's more like an outsider … nothing like he used to be."

"Oh? You mean he used to be nice? Wasn't always a bully?"

Freddy tossed small stones into the surf. He looked up into the sky. "Fog's finally burning off. Usually happens that way, you know? Foggy day, clear night. Who knows, maybe Bernie'll want us to go out after supper. Can't say I'd blame him. We're all losin' money this way."

Joanie huffed, her sparkling eyes signaling a teasing attitude. "So, Fred-dy, tell me about Pete. Has he always been a bully?" She leaned over to help Jessica build a sand castle. "Naw, he used to be lots of fun. When we were younger we were together a lot. Even though I was older. He was like a kid brother to me. Then his mom died about four or five years ago. Things went downhill fast. He started being mean to me and my little sisters, even to his friends. His dad couldn't do anything with him. And he started hanging out with some tough kids. Got in trouble more than once. Finally ended up in juvie."

"Juvie?"

"Yeah. Juvenile prison. I told you before."

"Did he blame himself for his mom's death?"

Freddy thought for a while. "Naw, I don't think so. She was killed in a car accident. Don't think he coulda felt to blame … but maybe. I don't know the whole story. Hal and Pete are both tight-lipped about the day it happened."

"What was your aunt like, Fred?"

"Real sweet. A good person. And after she died, Uncle Hal started going to her church. But Pete would have nothing to do with it. I can see that breaks my uncle's heart."

"I can imagine." Joanie remained quiet for a time.

Freddy respected her silence. He was surprised by her next words.

"There's a verse in the Bible that says that all things work together for good to them who love God. I believe that. I believe something good will come from this." Joanie turned to face him again. "You just wait and see." She smiled and leaned over to point with her cane at a bubble in the sand. "There, Jessica. Dig for the crab."

Freddy's guts told him nothing good would ever come from such a complicated mess. "Can't say I agree with you, Little Sis. Too much damage done. Pete's mad as a she-bear about to lose her cubs. He don't … doesn't want nobody … anybody stealing his dad's favor away from him. He lost his mom. He prob'ly thinks he's about to lose his dad, too."

Freddy doodled in the sand with the tip of Joanie's cane. He looked down, studying the incoming, splashing waves. His mind whirled like a waterspout, thinking about Pete. Angry, probably scared, probably lying about the net hole and the broken or cut tie-up rope, about killing seals—could he be trusted with anything? Did Freddy dare confront him about the seals, or should he tell Bernie? And if he did tell, how much trouble could Hal get into?

"And what about you, Fred? How is it with *your* family?"

Freddy sensed that Joanie knew he was hiding something. Did he dare tell her about Mattie? *She's fifteen going on twenty-five. She acts like she really cares. Maybe she won't get mad if I tell her. Can I count on her not telling anyone else … staying friends with me?*

"My dad left years ago," Freddy began after taking a deep breath. "He drank and beat me and Mom. At least he never touched my little sisters. Mattie … she's twelve now … always been stubborn. She's my favorite. One day when I was eleven … she was five … she begged Ma to have me take her swimming at the pool. When we got there, I started …"

"Jess!" Joanie rushed to her feet. "Where is she? Fred, where is she?"

Freddy's heart leaped into his throat at the muffled sound of Jessica's scream. Looking down, he discovered the tide had reached his boots. Frantic, he jumped up. "Jessica! We're coming!"

Freddy looked towards Hiding Rock. Another muffled sound reached his ears. Like a wild man, he tore down the shore. The tide rushed in, covering the beach. He stumbled but pushed on, uttering a breathless prayer. "Lord, let me reach her in time. Please, Lord, don't let her drown."

Jessica's cries became gurgles. Freddy took gigantic steps to the rock. Inside, the water had filled the cave. He stooped down, his head submerged, and reached forward. Groping frantically, he searched the water. "Please, Lord, please," he begged silently, without thought, while holding his breath. Then … just as he readied himself to back up for a breath of air, his hand snagged her shirt.

Grabbing for all he was worth, Freddy pulled her out as he half-stepped, half-swam backwards out of the cave. Once above water, he ran towards the upper beach, dropped Jessica to the ground, and stooped to listen for her breathing. Joanie, panting, fell to his side. She kept up a jerky, running prayer—half crying, half pleading for God's mercy.

Jessica gasped, her eyes wide with fear and panic. She choked a scream before vomiting a stream of sea water onto the beach.

Joanie stood and held out her trembling arms. "Come, Jessica," she pleaded with a shaky voice.

Jessica reached for Joanie, her wails winding down to whimpers. The three of them hurried back to Sitting Rock, Freddy holding Joanie's cane and supporting her elbow. Joanie sat rocking Jessica back and forth. Freddy sat next to them, wet and shaking.

"Let's get up to the cabin. Quick. She's cold." Freddy helped Joanie out of her jacket, at her insistence, to wrap around Jessica's shivering body. He grabbed his own wet jacket and wrung the sea water out of it before putting it on. His teeth chattered as he took a step to guide Joanie and Jessica up the hill. "How could I have been s-so s-stupid? It w-was my fault. I n-never get th-things right!"

Joanie turned to face him. "It wasn't your fault, Fred. It was mine. But ..." she sobbed, "I'm scared to tell Barb."

Nodding, Freddy turned his head at the familiar sound of crunching sand behind him. Pete! Wouldn't he ever leave them alone? He leered over them. Freddy's heart did a flip. How much had he seen? Or heard?

"I saw it all, Loser. And I'm gonna tell. You ..." he pointed to Joanie, "... You're in for big trouble when I do." With a loud, sneering laugh, he turned to leave.

Freddy tackled him from behind, wrapping his right arm around his neck. "You better not tell! It was an accident and you know it."

Pete threw Freddy over his shoulder. With a loud thud, Freddy landed on the wet sand. Pete grabbed him around the throat but Freddy managed a leg lock around his middle that released his hands. They rolled over and over in the sand right into the surf. They were an even match since Freddy had regained his strength.

Finally, with unspoken consent, they stopped fighting. Gasping, they came up for air. In mock surrender, Pete turned away. As he walked back towards his cabin, he turned around. "Looks like she can't keep a kid from almost drowning any more than you can. You two have something in common, Freddy ... you and your friend's crippled sister." With a sneer, he added, "Oh, excuse me. I mean my *brother's* crippled sister."

Joanie's face crumpled. She held Jessica out for Freddy to carry as they hurried up the hill. "What'll we do, Fred? Pete's right. It's all my fault. I don't want to be fired." Her squeaky voice turned into a sob.

Still puffing air but no longer shivering, Freddy put one free arm around her. "Don't worry, Little Sis. He might be all hot air. Let's just wait and see, okay? Besides, I can't imagine Barb firing you. Let's just get Jess to the cabin."

Freddy knew his own words were full of bravado. He also knew Pete was dead serious. If Pete actually did tear the hole in the net and cut the skiff line, he'd do about anything to get even. Freddy knew that for certain. *And though Barb obviously thinks a lot of Joanie, what about Bernie? He gets his shorts in a knot mighty fast sometimes. And they love Jessica to death.*

Freddy removed his arm from around Joanie's shoulder. "Get ahold of yourself, Little Sis. We don't want anyone else to see you upset."

She sniffed, placed a finger on one nostril, and blew snot in the sand.

"Oh, yuck! That's disgusting!" Freddy turned his head away. "Little Sis, for being an almost sweet-sixteen girl, and smart besides, you have the manners of a caveman. It's time to act like a young lady."

Joanie managed a laugh. At least it got her to stop crying, Freddy thought.

As they hurried up the walk, Freddy grew nervous. What would Bernie and Barb say when they returned from set-netting? He and Joanie looked beat up … to say nothing about Jessica. His thoughts weighed heavy. He felt it in his legs and arms but pretended everything was okay.

When they reached the hilltop, Freddy put Jessica down so she could run inside the cabin. "Feddy and me wet," she yelled to Jake and his parents. "Played by big rock."

Mr. B and Jake both looked up from their Monopoly game. But no one said anything. Freddy knew he and Joanie would have to wait it out.

Before Joanie had a chance to change Jessica's wet clothes for dry ones, Bernie and Barb returned from picking fish.

Freddy's heart fluttered. *They must have been right behind us. I wonder if they heard anything.*

"Feddy and me wet," she told her mother. "Played by big rock."

Barb scrunched down to face her. "What rock, honey?"

"Big rock. Got all wet … see?" Jessica patted herself. "All wet. Scary. Feddy put his ear by me … here." She touched her mouth.

Freddy held his breath. "We walked over to Hiding Rock and got too close to a big wave coming in. That's all. So we got soaked."

Would they believe this? Would they see that Joanie wasn't as wet as he and Jessica? His eye started to twitch as he waited for their reaction. Barb stood up and smiled. Bernie stood, stared at Freddy. *Oh-oh, here it comes.* But Bernie smiled, too, giving Joanie an affectionate pat on her back.

"Just be careful, okay?" is all he said.

Freddy turned his head so Bernie wouldn't hear the air releasing from his lips.

Bernie hung up his float coat and pants. "Barb and I decided we'll have an early supper and hit the hay. Looks like it's been strenuous enough on most of us. We'll get an early start tomorrow." He touched Freddy's shoulder. "We'll take Jake's dad out with us, if he wants to ride along."

Later in their tent, Freddy lay wide awake. "So how you feelin', Jake? Wanna talk?"

"Guess so. I'm too mad to sleep yet." Jake hesitated so long, Freddy wondered if he'd fallen asleep anyway—until he heard Jake grinding his teeth.

"What Mom told me is like the worst soap opera ever! I still can hardly believe it." Jake turned to lean on his elbow. "She and Hal were married, but Hal drank some. One night when he came home half-drunk, she had the table set for a celebration dinner. She was gonna tell him she was expecting a baby … me."

Freddy couldn't deny the sob that came from Jake's lips. "If you wanna talk later, that's okay, Jake."

"No, that's okay. Gotta get this out. Anyway, Hal wasn't in the mood for a celebration and he shoved Mom a little. She got upset and threw him out.

"Next thing she knew, her family in Wisconsin persuaded her to file for divorce. Apparently Mom's family had never liked Hal anyway. So she went ahead with the divorce and moved back to Wisconsin. That's where I was born.

"While there, she met my dad … I mean Wendall. He was a chaplain, and because of him, Mom had a 'spiritual awakening,' she called it. He was older, more stable, and they got married. Before I was born, in fact.

"Mom said it all happened so fast, she sort of put her life with Hal behind her. They decided they'd tell me about my real dad when I got to be five. Not that it would have mattered, they decided."

"Why not?" Freddy asked.

"Because Mom had gotten a letter from Hal's mother saying he'd drowned."

Freddy cringed at the irony of Jake's story. He took a deep breath and let it out in a whistle. "Why didn't she check out the story?"

"That's what I asked Mom." Jake went on after a ragged sob escaped his lips. "The truth is, after Hal met his second wife he quit drinking and went back to fishing. He did almost drown during a fishing trip. Sounds like Hal's family didn't like Mom much, and that's why his mom wrote the letter. To make sure she was totally out of the picture, I guess."

"If it was me, I'd feel like killin' 'em," Freddy growled. "Bet you do too."

"Yeah, maybe I do."

Freddy's forehead creased downward. "I still don't get why your mom didn't check on the story."

"She'd made a new life—a happy life—for herself and me, and later Joanie. She didn't want anything more to do with Alaska." Jake remained silent for a while.

"Now I get it!" he burst out. "When we moved to Alaska three years ago, she didn't want to go. So that's why! I remember one day before we moved, she called herself 'an obedient Christian wife.' Said she'd go anywhere with Dad … um, Wendall. She didn't act very happy, though. You know, about moving. But we came to Alaska."

"Are you glad you did?"

"Of course. What's not to like about Alaska?" Jake's chuckle sounded forced to Freddy's ears.

Freddy snorted. "Williwaws, that's what."

"You're right about that. But … it's gonna take some getting used to being your cousin." Jake jabbed Freddy in the chest.

"I know the feeling." Freddy jabbed him back. In the dim light of the tent, he glimpsed Jake rolling onto his back, hands behind his head.

"Seriously, much as I hate to admit it, I'm trying to believe that God has a reason for all this. And I have to remember to love my enemies. Meaning Pete. It won't be easy. But … like Dad, I mean Wendall keeps telling me, God will be there for me."

"Huh! Mighta known you'd get religious on me. I've heard enough. Good night, Jake."

Freddy lay still long after Jake's soft snores permeated the tent. *Wish I had his faith. He's right. It ain't gonna be easy, with Pete on his case even more than before. I'll have to watch out for him. I don't think God can do that all by Himself.*

## *Chapter 11*

# THE BEAR

The weather took a good turn, remaining sunny and calm for more than a week. In fact, Mr. B felt well enough to join the crew several times. Freddy noticed that during much of Mr. B's time in the skiff, he simply enjoyed the fresh air and give-and-take joking with the crew. But he also took his nitroglycerin pills more often.

One day, unaware he was staring, Freddy felt his face heat up when Mr. B winked at him.

"No sense in me hiding my meds ... like you trying to hide your scar. You don't kid me, Freddy, the way you keep your head turned so we don't notice. What was it? A cleft palate surgery gone wrong?"

*Usually nobody gets away with mentionin' my scar. But ... how can I be mad at Mr. B? He means well.*

"Yeah. I don't talk much about it."

Mr. B turned serious. "You don't have to hide behind a scar. It's not who you are. Look beyond the scar, Son, even when others won't."

Freddy swallowed a sudden thickening in his throat. He nodded, tried to smile.

Mr. B continued. "I have a feeling you're hiding more scars inside than the one on your lips. Right?"

*How does he know? Is he psychic? What am I s'posed to say?* Freddy turned away, focusing on Jake instead. And by the looks of Jake's tight-lipped expression, he too was well aware that his dad was sick. Either that or he still felt the effects of Hal and his mom's news.

Freddy agreed with Jake about one thing. Pete was keeping to himself. That meant a more relaxed time spent picking fish in spite of the long, hard hours they put in. But Freddy missed spending time with Joanie. He felt drawn to her because of her cheerful smile and optimism. He always had the urge to protect her … like he did for his sister, Mattie, after the accident. That's why he kept an eye out for her even while he fished offshore.

One evening Barb made an announcement. "They called in a twenty-four-hour closure," she said. "We need to move the outhouse, but we'll have to wait for a longer closure." She grinned at the men. "Not that you're unhappy to put off digging a new hole and moving the biffy, of course."

Before anyone could respond, Joanie looked at Freddy with pleading eyes. "Can we go check out the wildflowers tomorrow?" She turned her gaze to Barb. "While Jessica takes her nap?"

Barb smiled. "Sure, Joanie. Take the afternoon off. You deserve a break, too."

The next day proved as sunny and calm as previous days. After lunch, Joanie grabbed her sketching supplies, stuffing everything in her backpack. "Beat you to Sitting Rock, Fred." She threw her backpack at him.

"Oof!" Before he recovered from her hard, underhanded throw, she ran out the cabin door and down the hill, barely using her cane. Freddy didn't catch up to her until they reached the rock. "Hey, Little Sis! You're getting better and better at walking. Didn't know you had it in you." He gave her a high-five as she stood catching her breath.

Smiling, Joanie looked all around, pointed towards a grassy meadow beyond the cabin, and said, "There, Fred. Let's go up there. Won't there be lots of wildflowers?"

"Sure. Let's go." He walked beside her, carrying her backpack, glad to be on solid ground for a whole day.

When they reached a small field of colorful wildflowers, Joanie stopped. "They're beautiful. You have to tell me about every one." She opened the backpack and set up her portable easel and supplies. Kneeling on the soft grass, she began to sketch first one flower, then another. "Okay, Teach, what are they? I have to identify them on my sketches or I'll forget."

Freddy pointed to a large patch of short, delicate flowers. "'Course you know about our state flower, right?"

"Of course. The Forget-Me-Not."

"They're called Alpine Forget-Me-Nots. In a couple weeks, the ground will be covered with them. All over the state."

"My mom dries them for decoration. They're so dainty. And they use them for so many things. I've even tasted Forget-Me-Not honey. And tea."

Freddy scanned the ground for other flowers. "It's a little early for some wildflowers. In a couple weeks we'll see the Alaska Cotton plant."

"Yeah, they're cool with their soft, hairy heads. They look exactly like cotton balls."

While Joanie ,sketched, Freddy kept up a running commentary on Alaskan plants.

"I'm amazed at your expertise, Fred. Where did you learn about all this? And … by the way, your grammar is improving every day. I'm proud of you." Joanie squinted into the sunlight, a wide smile creasing her face.

Freddy shrugged. "I've always been interested in nature. Just picked it up along the way, I guess. Don't mean to change the subject, but … your dad is getting worse, isn't he? I can see it every day. Have you talked to your mom about it?"

Joanie's lips tightened, her eyes shining with unshed tears. "Y-yes. She told Jake and me that as soon as they go home in another week or so, he's going to see his cardiologist again. They'll probably set him up for a heart bypass. She said he's in God's hands and not to worry. But I can see the worry on her face more than on his."

Joanie turned away. "I hate to think about it. I'm scared for him. Yet I know his faith is rock solid. I thought mine was, too, until now. And with this new development, the stress about Jake being Hal's son … it seems like everything is falling apart. This can't be helping Dad's heart."

"Yeah, it's gotta be hard. But … think about it, Little Sis. You'll be my shirt-tail cousin! Can't argue with that, can you? Means we'll see more of each other. Means I can tease you more." Freddy gave her arm a playful punch.

Joanie's smile returned. "Nope, can't argue with that, Fred."

Freddy jumped at a sound behind them. Gasping, he threw Joanie down to the ground. "Sh-h, it's a brown bear. Don't utter a sound," he whispered, sprawling on top of her.

Easel and pencils and tablet flew. Freddy's ear jammed into Joanie's chin. Beneath him, the edge of her backpack poked his arm. He closed his eyes and tried to catch his breath; Joanie's came as fast as a field mouse fleeing an eagle.

"S-stay quiet. Maybe it-it'll leave," Freddy whispered. His arm tightened as he felt the grizzly sniffing it. *Lord, we need You. Quick! I'll do anything You say, just get this bear off of us.*

Joanie moaned a prayer under her breath and then whispered, "How much longer? I'm suffocating."

Freddy dared not move. "Not yet," he whispered back as the bear huffed, its rotten breath near Freddy's neck. With a giant claw, it raked the backpack, shredding it and grazing Freddy's exposed arm. He sucked in his breath as he felt warm blood seeping down onto the ground.

Freddy lost track of time. They lay there terrified. The bear panted, its breath just inches from Freddy's head as it continued to ravage the backpack. Freddy squeezed his eyes shut harder and waited ….

After an eternity, the Kodiak bear quit tearing the backpack. Freddy heard its footsteps slowly retreat. He waited, his heart still pounding, and then inch by agonizing inch, he moved his head until he glimpsed it loping away. "Let's get out of here," he whispered. He eased himself off Joanie's shaking body.

"You-you're hurt, Fred. Let me look," Joanie said, grabbing a rag from the trampled ground. "Here. It's from my art kit. Let's wrap it around your arm. Hurry. Give me my cane. Let's go."

Freddy didn't argue. They half-ran back to the cabin, both turning around often to make sure the bear didn't come back.

Joanie burst into the cabin door. "Call the Fish and Game! Tell them they have to move that bear … it almost killed us."

The cabin silence shattered as everyone scraped their chairs trying to reach Freddy and Joanie. Mrs. B's face went white at the sight of Freddy's bleeding arm. Barb gasped when she saw his wound. She led him over to her first aid kit and began cleaning his gash.

Freddy's voice shook. "Aw, it's just a scratch, Boss Lady. I'll be fine."

Joanie snorted. "Yeah, right. Big he-man here. You should have seen him, Dad. He was shaking as hard as I was. But …. " her voice dropped to a whisper. "… he saved my life."

As they told the story, Bernie reported the bear over his CB radio, loudly protesting their law about not removing nuisance or dangerous bears from the area. The reply crackled with a loud protest in return. Bernie mumbled a few words and rang off.

"Seems this is a different bear. Something is bringing them down this way, that's for sure. Boys, you'd better bring your sleeping bags in again. Sorry. And we'd all better be on guard from now on. Although since we burn our garbage, it's unlikely it'll be back."

No one left the cabin the rest of the day. They all kept looking at the closed door. Freddy didn't agree with Bernie. He wondered not if, but when, the bear would return. He wondered what it would take for a grizzly to break through their cabin door if it really wanted to. He hoped Barb's good food smells didn't draw the bear back again. The only things that eased the tension of the event came from a long game of Monopoly and Jessica's usual hilarity.

Crash! Everyone jumped when the door slammed open.

*Chapter 12*

# PETE SNITCHES

Pete charged inside. Hands on hips, he reached Bernie in two strides.

Bernie glared at him. "You can't come charging in here like this. What's the matter with you? Get out!"

Pete sneered. "You won't be saying that after I tell you about your baby girl."

*Uh-oh. Here it comes. Joanie's in for it now.* Freddy rushed next to Joanie when he heard her sharp intake of breath.

Bernie's chiseled face remained set like stone. "Tell me what? Out with it, and it better not be lies. Or I'll see that your dad pulls you out of camp pronto. Got it?"

Pete's sneer grew into a harsh laugh. "Remember the day they came in all wet? Well, that's because Joanie almost let your baby drown at Hiding Rock." He stepped back to glare at Joanie and Freddy before turning Bernie's way again. "Didn't know she was so careless, did you?"

Barb gasped, her hand flying to her mouth.

Bernie's face tightened. He pushed Freddy away and grabbed Joanie's arm. He looked at her then at Pete. "Get out now, Pete. This is between me and her." He banged the door open for Pete to leave.

Jake's gaze caught Freddy's. "What's Pete got against my sister? Just because she's a girl? With a cane?"

"Don't know." Freddy turned to Bernie. "It wasn't her fault, Boss. Let me explain. We were just talkin' an' I got her sidetracked. It was my fault, not hers."

"What was your fault? I thought you said … you lied to me, Freddy! What really happened?"

Freddy explained how they missed seeing Jessica leave Joanie's side, how the tide came in, and how they didn't realize it until Jessica cried.

"H-he was a hero, Bernie," Joanie interrupted. "He s-saved Jess's life … he almost got hypothermia going in the cave and pulling her out. He-he only …."

Bernie's face crumpled. He squeezed his eyes shut. "Boys, I'll handle this from here on. Joanie, let's take a little walk."

"But …." Freddy panicked. Would Bernie harm her?

"Don't worry. We're just going to have a talk. Leave us be."

Freddy and Jake watched helplessly as Bernie left the cabin with Joanie following. Freddy couldn't help but notice tears streaming down Joanie's eyes. His own eyes welled up thinking about it.

His mind whirled. Sorrow for Joanie. Anger at Pete. Confusion about why it even happened. Grinding his teeth in frustration, he mumbled, "I oughta kill him for this."

Jake jerked his head up, surprise written on his face. "No, Freddy. That's not the way to handle it. Let Bernie take care of it. Pete will get his in the end, just wait and see. It's not up to us to do the punishing."

"But … what if Bernie fires her? And speaking about wanting to kill, not that long ago you said guess you'd like to kill your family. Remember?"

"Well, I've been doing some hard thinking since then."

"And?"

Jake plunked down on the couch. "You don't want to hear me say it." He grinned sheepishly.

"Try me."

"Well, I got to thinking what Jesus would want me to do. You know. Forgive Mom and Hal. Even if my gut tells me different sometimes. Even if I'd like to run away forever sometimes. Even if … yeah, even if I'd like to kill them both sometimes." Jake choked out his words so Freddy barely understood them. "God wants me to love them."

Freddy's throat thickened. He patted his jeans pocket, the one that held his lucky jackknife. the knife he had felt like using on Pete more than once these past weeks.

Maybe there was more to Jake's God than Freddy thought. Could he learn to love Pete again? And how about himself? He shook his head.

Deep in thought, Freddy almost missed Joanie's laugh as she and Bernie came through the door. Bernie had his arm draped across her shoulder.

Freddy blinked. "Well, I'll be …." He whispered as he jabbed Jake's leg. "Do you believe it?"

Jake jumped up, a smile creasing his face. "So everything's okay?"

"Nothing wrong," Bernie said. "Let's eat. I smell good food."

Freddy looked at Jake and shrugged. Bernie wasn't going to tell them anything. They'd have to get it out of Joanie later. They could bide their time. As long as Joanie had her smile back, that was all that counted. For now.

## *Chapter 13*

# PICNIC TIME

The next ten days dragged. With near-gale winds from the southeast, intermittent rain, and tangles in the nets, Freddy couldn't wait for the next closure. The fishing was good, but was it worth the dangerous, agonizing work? Worth the long hours pulling the nets against battering seas and rushing tides? Worth trying not to spill overboard with every wave while picking salmon through the nets?

Jake's face clearly showed his struggle against seasickness. Freddy noticed, however, that as long as his friend kept his eyes on the shoreline, he didn't vomit. He knew that a mere quarter mile from shore could be as hard on the gut as ten miles, for guys prone to seasickness like Jake.

When the next closure was announced, the weather cleared. "Wouldn't you know?" Bernie groused inside the cabin one morning. "Why can't they schedule the closures for bad weather and fishing during the good?"

Barb laughed. "You oughta know fishing by now, Bernie. Anyway, you promised we could go to the lagoon for a picnic during the next closure. Moving the outhouse can wait, can't it? Why don't we go tomorrow first thing? We'll have the whole day to relax."

Sarah and Wendall expressed delight along with Jake and Joanie when Bernie agreed with his wife. Freddy tickled Jessica into a giggling fit. "We're glad, too … aren't we, Jess?"

She giggled some more. "Go on pinnick! Go on pinnick!" she hollered over and over as she raced around the room.

The cabin became awash in plans for the picnic. Barb and Joanie prepared fish sandwiches and three-bean salad which they stored in the generator-cooled fridge. They also set all the necessary picnic gear on the table for the next day. Rather than take showers that night, Jake and Freddy decided to wait, and bathe in the warm lagoon water.

In spite of their exhaustion from ten days of hard fishing, Freddy and Jake joined in the lively chatter. Not only would the day provide rest for their tired bodies, but it would be a stress-free time away from Pete and the emotional trauma revolving around him and Hal.

During breakfast, Bernie radioed in for an updated weather report. "Looks good all day. A stiff southwest breeze, but sunny. One thing, though. The tides are high so we have to be mindful of that going through the inlet to the lagoon."

"How narrow is the inlet?" Jake asked. "I'll never forget the one we went through on our way to the Pribilof Islands last winter. Narrow enough to make our boat rock like a bucking bronco. But this one shouldn't be a big deal, right? Even in our little skiff?"

Bernie grabbed an armful of food containers. "Right. As long as we respect the movement of the water. Tidal currents ripping through the channel make for big waves."

Once everyone finished carrying the food and gear to the skiff, Bernie made an announcement. "Barb, you and Joanie and Jess will ride with me in my new holding skiff. Freddy, you take me out to get it. You use this one and take Jake and his parents. You'll be the navigator. You know the way to the lagoon, right?"

"Sure, Boss," Freddy said. "Been there before. Let's go while the tide's right." *Sure glad Jake's mom and dad will be together. They need this, what with the big change in Jake's life. But I wish Bernie had given me the bigger skiff. He treats it like a kid with a new toy too jealous to let anybody else touch it.*

Once both skiffs were loaded, Bernie led the way. In spite of the nice day, the constant breeze against the tide brought choppy waves coming in fast. The bow of Freddy's skiff slapped down hard. One slap after another. A quick glance at Mrs. B alarmed Freddy. Her face turned white and her throat convulsed. *Uh-oh. Sure hope she doesn't have to puke. It's no fun being seasick, especially on a picnic.*

The skiffs finally motored around a curve into a quiet bay that led to the inlet Bernie warned about. But slack tide allowed them to glide through on the narrow and now-calm shelf of water into the lagoon. Freddy felt relieved when color came back into Mrs. B's cheeks.

He took his time motoring along the big lagoon. He scanned the shoreline, a perfect bowl broken only by two short docks, one on each side.

Bernie had already tied his larger skiff to the dock on their left. Freddy tied up behind him and his crew helped unload all the picnic gear. Jake helped Freddy carry Barb's big cooler a ways down the narrow beach where a cluster of willows offered shade next to a small stream. They shoved the cooler under one of the trees.

"Come on, gang! Let's get ready for clam digging," Bernie called. "Freddy, do you have a sport license to dig?"

"Yep. An' here's my rake." He pulled a short-handled, four-tined metal rake from his gear bag and, grinning, held up his orange bibs. With a flourish, he stepped into them and pulled them up, right over his jeans. "This is a serious job for the knees," he told Jake and Joanie. "Don't wanna get holes in my jeans." He fell onto his knees, pretending to look for clams before standing again. "Too early. Tide has to go out a ways."

"Feddy look funny," Jessica said. She giggled, falling down and digging in the sand with her toy rake. When her hand touched a pink sea star, her face radiated with wonder. She tried to grasp the creature with her small, pudgy fingers, grunted, and ran to Barb. "Help me, Mama. See the petty fishy?"

Bernie and Barb sat cross-legged on the narrow beach to play with Jessica while Jake's parents set up a pair of Bernie's lawn chairs in a spot of sunshine near the dock.

"Ah, no wind!" Jake threw his arms open and jumped into the air. "I didn't realize how windy it is every day back on Eagle Point."

Freddy threw a stick into the retreating tide. "Yeah. Sure is nice here." While waiting for the tide to continue ebbing, he meandered along the beach, picking up bits of oddly-shaped driftwood and seashells, carrying his ten-gallon pail and rake. "C'mon, you guys. Let's walk."

Jake and Joanie joined him, Joanie running to catch up. "I forgot my cane, guys. Wait up!"

"Aw, you don't need it any more, do you?" Freddy waited for her. "You're doing so well."

Jake agreed. "Soon you won't need it at all, Sis."

Joanie snorted. "We'll see. But the Lord has brought me this far, I'll say that. You agree, Freddy?"

*Will she never shut up about God?* "Guess so," he mumbled. As he led the way around the curve of the lagoon, Freddy heard a boat motor. He squinted, shading his eyes with both hands. "Uh-oh, here comes trouble, Jake."

Hal and Pete, instead, pulled up to the far dock in one of their skiffs and kept to themselves. Freddy could see that they had come specifically to dig for clams. Maybe Pete would leave them alone this time.

Freddy cleared his throat. "So, Little Sis. What did Bernie have to say about … you know … about Jessica and Hiding Rock? Sure didn't look like he canned you. He didn't, did he?"

"No." Joanie's mouth turned upward a notch. "He was real nice. He said he should fire me, and really gave it to me for not watching Jess close enough. But he's giving me another chance … and I'd better remember that. He ended his lecture by actually hugging me. Can you believe it?" She gave her brother a shove. "Must be my charm, huh, Jake?"

Jake smiled in return. "Yeah, I think you've got him and Barb both wrapped around your little finger. You lucked out, Sis."

Joanie blushed. "Well … they know how much I love watching Jessica. And they really are nice people. Even Bernie. He's gruff sometimes, and let's face it. I deserved his harsh words. Especially since Barb told me he's under a lot of stress for having to take out a loan for that new skiff."

The three kept walking and talking until Freddy said, "The tide's out enough to start digging clams. This looks like a good spot." He dropped to his knees and began to dig in the sand.

Joanie watched him intently. "How can you see where they are, Fred? I don't see anything."

Grunting, he said, "Look for little bubbles. That's where you'll find a clam." He dug through a bubble in the sand, pulling up a clam. "See? Like so."

After an hour of fast digging, Freddy stopped to carry the pail to the dock. He pulled out another pail and began to dig for more clams. Jake and Joanie were not allowed to dig since they had no license, so as Freddy continued, they spent time with their parents back at the picnic area. Before they realized, it was time to eat lunch.

"Do pinnick!" Jessica announced. "Do pinnick, Feddy!" She ran over to where he knelt on the beach's edge. "Eat pinnick, Feddy. Now!"

Freddy laughed as he stood up. Stretching stiff muscles, he set the second pail full next to the first. "Okay, Jess. Let's eat pinnick … now." He caught her up, swung her around, and deposited her at her mother's side.

Jessica giggled and screeched. "You funny, Feddy."

After Barb and Joanie set the picnic lunch on a tablecloth over the sand, Mr. B offered a short prayer of thanks. Then they began eating Barb's salmon sandwiches and three-bean salad topped off with her famous double chocolate cake. They ate their fill with relish, taking leisure advantage of the fresh, warm air of the lagoon. Freddy was especially glad to see Mr. and Mrs. B enjoying the day with Jake. Their laughter echoed across the lagoon.

After the meal, Mr. and Mrs. B dozed in the sunshine along with Jessica. Even Barb and Joanie napped while Freddy and Bernie kept digging for clams.

Jake made his way over to Freddy. "Man, you reek! You need a bath, Freddy." He gave Freddy a shove hard enough to make him fall head first onto the wet sand. "Last one in is a skinned salmon." He danced away.

"Wait! No fair, I'm not ready." Freddy shucked off his bibs and boots and ran into the water.

Apparently hearing their splashing, Joanie and Jessica followed. The four of them cavorted in the warm, clear water while scrubbing themselves clean with sand from the bottom of the lagoon.

Freddy, the first to leave, returned to his clam digging. He had barely covered the bottom of his pail before he looked up when he heard Hal's skiff motor. Hal waved as they turned the skiff towards the inlet.

Bernie looked up, too. "We'd better get going. We don't want to miss that slack tide." He gathered the picnic gear, collected his passengers, and helped them into his new holding skiff.

Freddy kept digging. "You go ahead, Bernie. We'll be right behind you. I'm gonna keep digging. Gotta get at least another half a pail full. The limit's a thousand a day, you know. Not sure I'll get that many, but gonna try."

"Don't make it too long, Freddy." Bernie jerked on the engine cord, revved the motor, and left the dock in a cloud of oil smoke that hung in the air.

*Chapter 14*

# OVERBOARD!

Freddy's pail filled slowly. He worked faster, sweat dripping from his face. He looked up at Jake. "Sure wish you could help."

"Half a pail full or not, we should be going," Jake said. "I'm jittery enough on tide water. I don't like galloping boats any more than galloping horses."

Freddy sighed. "Yeah, yeah. Don't get your shorts in a knot." He stood up. "Guess we might as well leave."

With a sinking feeling, Freddy noticed that the beach had grown much wider. He groaned and muttered to himself as he started the engine.

"What's that you say?" Jake asked.

"Oh, just wishing we had the holding skiff instead of this shorter one. It'd get us through the inlet easier."

Jake sputtered. "Now you tell us! Is it too late? Shouldn't we wait for the next tide?"

"Naw, we'll make it through okay. We just hafta hang on tight. Hear that, Mr. and Mrs. B?"

Mr. B nodded. He grabbed his wife's hand as they stepped into the skiff.

Freddy motored slowly towards the inlet. What they saw ahead made them all gasp. The water gathered in millions of tiny bubbles that fizzled under the surface and then burst to the top in white foam. *Reminds me of a tub full of fizzy pop ready to explode.*

The closer they drew to the inlet, the faster the water moved under them. With a whoosh, they were in the inlet. Freddy was shocked to see that the water on each side of the narrow shelf had dropped a good foot or more. The shelf, no longer calm, looked like a menacing demon.

Freddy's palms grew sweaty on the tiller. "Hang on, Mrs. B!" He knew she couldn't hear him. The rushing water sounded like a waterfall. The skiff bucked from side to side until Freddy feared they'd tip over ... just like a mini-version of the williwaw tipping the *Danny Boy* ninety degrees.

Frantic to steer the light skiff ramrod straight along the very center of the narrow shelf, but worried about Jake and his parents, he dared to glance up at them. Jake sat in the bow, tight-lipped, trying to hold his mother's shoulders down. The skiff rocked and bucked and then ... a scream ... a loud splash ... a collective gasp.

"Mrs. B!" Freddy's scream shattered the wind.

"Help," Jake's mom called weakly as she tumbled like a rag doll in the churning water. Jake dove in after her.

"Lord, help us!" Mr. B cried out. "Save my wife."

With Mr. B's plea, Freddy instantly cut the throttle. Already the skiff had reached the end of the surging inlet. "Mr. B, come over here. Hurry!" Freddy yelled. "Take the tiller. We're on idle. Just keep us off the rocks. I'm gonna help Jake."

Mr. B, ashen-faced, took over the steering. The water still boiled, but at least they were off the shelf.

Freddy jumped into the cold, churning water. The roaring tide kept pulling him under as he fought to reach the top. His struggles to find air and to avoid the skiff's motor hampered his search for Mrs. B. Seconds turned to hours in his mind. Finally able to scan the water, he saw her. *There! But where's Jake? Lord, don't let them die. Please."* He swam to Mrs. B who was fighting to stay afloat. She appeared limp, ready to give up. Freddy swam hard towards her but, even with a life jacket on, the churning water kept pulling him under.

Just as he finally reached her, Jake came up next to him. Freddy grabbed Mrs. B under the arms. "Help me, Jake," he gasped. "... water's too rough."

Jake held onto his mom's life jacket. Between them, they managed to pull her to the skiff. It took both of them to push her inside as Mr. B tried to steady it. By now, Freddy was hyperventilating, clinging to starboard.

Visions of Jessica's submerged body competed with the picture of his sister, Mattie, lying face down in the swimming pool. Would he forever be reminded of it? *Why, God? Why do you keep setting me up with people who are drowning? Haven't I done enough?* With super-human effort, he pulled himself into the skiff. Without realizing it, he began to sob.

"Freddy!" Mr. B's voice punctured his memories. "She's breathing. Take over here so I can help her."

Freddy had to make sure. He swiped at his tears then squinted, watching to see that her chest rose and fell. Relief washed over him. Taking the tiller once more, he let Mr. B and Jake lay Mrs. B down on the wet bottom of the skiff.

"She's unconscious," Mr. B said. "Must have hit a rock. Look at this gash."

Blood oozed from a wide cut on her head, mixing to a pink tinge with water that dripped from her hair.

"Let's hurry, Freddy," Mr. B said. "We don't want her getting hypothermia. Wish we had that picnic blanket that Bernie took back with him."

Freddy kept the throttle wide open all the way back. Though the wind followed them, it was a rough ride. All Freddy heard was the roar of the motor. But he couldn't avoid the sight of Mr. B's lips moving in constant prayer, or the sight of tears coursing down his cheeks. Jake's head found his dad's shoulder for a time; his whole body shook. Between them, they kept pressure on Mrs. B's gash as they tried to keep her upper torso out of the water that sloshed on the skiff bottom.

Freddy allowed the skiff to fly on the strong wind. It rose and fell in a lulling rhythm, speaking to Freddy. Hurry, hurry, it said, as Jake and his dad gripped the sides of the boat while seeing to Mrs. B. Every few seconds Freddy glanced their way, making sure everyone was okay.

Midway back to Eagle Point, Mr. B turned white as the belly of a halibut. His hands shook as he clutched his chest, gasping for air. He suddenly leaned over and shuddered.

Like a horror movie, Freddy watched the scene unfold, his hand on autopilot as it guided the skiff through the sea. Jake struggling with one hand to keep Mr. B from falling. Mr. B patting his jacket pocket. Jake digging in the pocket, retrieving a small bottle. Prying the cover open while keeping his mother propped up between his knees. Pouring a tiny pill in his shaking hand. Holding Mr. B's head up, gently pushing the pill between his clenched teeth. Leaning over to dip his hand in the sea water. Filling his hand, bringing it to Mr. B's mouth. The desperation in Jake's eyes as he turned towards the stern made Freddy's own eyes fill.

"Freddy, slow down!" Jake screamed. "Dad, you can't die on me! You can't! If Mom dies, who'll be there for me?"

Freddy shook his head as if to rid himself of the unfolding tragedy. He wanted to slow the skiff, to ease the jarring of the boat on Mrs. B's body. But he dare not. Time wouldn't wait. They had to get back soon. *No more, God. Mattie in the pool, Jessica at Hiding Rock, Mom's cancer, the Danny Boy going down. How can I take any more? How can Jake take any more? What if his parents die? And Joanie—what would she do? It's not fair, God! Hear me? It's not fair. Do You even care? But I'm begging. Please ... please don't let them die. It's my fault ... I shoulda made Bernie let me take the bigger skiff.*

Freddy dragged his jacket sleeve across his face and once more turned towards his three passengers. At that instant, with a jerk Mr. B sat up, color quickly returning to his cheeks. Freddy let out a long, shuddering breath of relief. He looked upward. *Thank You.*

They finally reached Eagle Point. After Freddy secured the skiff, he helped Mr. B out and guided him up the hill. Jake carried his mother in his arms.

"Take it easy, Mr. B." Freddy, aware of the sick man's heavy breathing, tried to be gentle as he pulled on his arm. He wanted to hurry Mr. B to the warm cabin but knew he was in no condition to hurry. "You'll both soon be okay." *If only that can be true.*

Ahead, Jake kicked at the cabin door. Joanie opened the door, shrieked, looked towards Freddy, and shrieked again. "What happened?"

Quiet confusion took over the cabin. By the time Joanie and Barb had changed Mrs. B's wet clothes for dry and had laid her on the sofa under a ton of blankets, Mr. B sat comfortably next to her. After Freddy and Jake dashed to their tent to change into dry clothes, things began to settle down. Bernie and Barb helped with the care of Mr. and Mrs. B while they debated calling the Coast Guard.

Freddy's gaze burned into Mrs. B as if it would magically cause her to move. Despair shook his whole body. *Oh God, I beg You, make her move!*

And then … the blankets wiggled. An arm moved. A hand opened. Eyes opened, glazed but open. Mrs. B grimaced, drew her hand up to her head, groaned.

Joanie, sitting on the floor by her dad, smoothed her mother's hair, whispering soft words. Barb stirred a pot of hot broth and brought a cup to Mrs. B. She spoon-fed her until her shivering stopped. Mrs. B's eyes opened and closed several times before she squinted and looked around the room.

A collective sigh echoed throughout the cabin.

Mr. B closed his eyes. "Thank You, Lord God. Thank You."

*Chapter 15*

# A TALK WITH MR. B

Freddy's emotions churned like the rushing tide at the lagoon inlet. "I'm going out," he mumbled.

"Wait, Fred! I'll go with you." Joanie rose abruptly from her chair to follow.

Freddy turned. "No. Leave me alone … please." He hurried out the door. Inside the tent, he threw himself down on his sleeping bag, folded his hands behind his head, and stared at the ceiling. How could he have made such a stupid mistake? He almost let Mrs. B drown. It could have been the end of Mr. B, too. Why did he wait so long to leave the lagoon? His breath came in short, quick puffs as he squeezed his eyes shut.

Hearing a scratch at the door, he opened his eyes, squinted. Mr. B. *Leave me alone, everybody.* He turned to face the tent wall.

"Mind if I come in? I know you're thinking it was your fault. But there's more, isn't there, Freddy? More hurt. Want to talk about it?"

Freddy gave his head a slight shake.

Mr. B's unwanted presence filled the tent. "You know, I've been a chaplain for many years. One thing I've learned, it doesn't do any good holding it in. Once the hurt is out, that's when the healing begins. I've seen it happen hundreds of times. Care to try, Freddy? I promise it'll stay between you and me, and I promise not to judge."

Freddy felt the turmoil clear to his booted toes. His mind raced. Should he? What would he gain? Could he banish the nightmares, the endless mind-pictures of Mattie that tormented him? Of Jessica? And now of Mrs. B? *Three times and out, they say. Does that mean next time someone will actually drown? Will I always be such a loser?*

Mr. B touched Freddy's shoulder. "This is eating you up. Tell me about it. Nothing's as bad as you think."

Freddy exploded from his bed. "Nothing, huh? Wanna bet? What about watching your mom go through chemo? What about being forced to watch my dad beat my mom? What about almost letting my own sister drown? What about almost letting her have brain damage? What about disappointing my ma when I failed Mattie? And Jessica. God, I almost let her drown, too! That's not bad, you're tellin' me?" Freddy sank back on his bed, covering his face with his hands. His body shook with sobs.

Freddy felt Mr. B's persistent but gentle touch again as the man knelt beside him. He forced Freddy's head around to look him square in the eye. "You keep saying the word Almost. Almost is like the words What If. We can't live out the What Ifs.

"Listen, my friend. Nothing is too hard for God. Nothing. He's seen it all. He knows every thought you have, hears every word you say, sees everything you do. And He still loves you. He even counts every hair on your head."

Freddy's eyes stung. He wiped his nose with his shirt sleeve and took a deep breath. "How do you know? How can that be? If only …." His voice dropped to a whisper. "I'm afraid."

"Let God take away your fear, Freddy. Let Him replace it with faith. Believe that He can do it. God's love is for everyone … no matter how horrible their life is. I've seen it again and again, as a chaplain. I've counseled murderers, rapists, addicts, you name it. When they come to realize the truth of God's love for them, it changes them. It can change you, too, Freddy."

"B-but I almost let them die! I should have …."

"No. Things happen. You can't fix everything. That's what you've been doing all along. Right? Trying to cover up your guilty feelings by saving everyone?"

"I'm to blame, Mr. B. It's always my fault."

"Freddy, you're not God. Don't even try to be. It won't get you anywhere. You should know that by now."

Mr. B touched the scar on Freddy's lip. "Look beyond the scar, my friend. Look past the scars of hurt and guilt that are growing harder. They're keeping you from enjoying life as God meant you to.

"Sin has consequences and leaves scars. You don't have to forget what happened, but you can let God do His work. When we ask His forgiveness, He forgets our sins. He wants you to start thinking about the good things God has given you. Your family's love. Your intelligence. Your expertise in fishing. And your gift of teaching. God has blessed you with many talents."

Freddy touched his scar, feeling the ridge beneath his fingers. Touching it seemed foreign to him. He usually tried to avoid even looking at it.

After long moments, he took a deep, shuddering breath and stood up. "Thanks, Mr. B. I'm gonna take a walk now, if you don't mind."

"Sure, Son. Just remember, God loves you. Nothing is too hard for Him. He *always* looks beyond the scars. In fact, He heals them. I'm not talking about the scar on your lip. I'm talking about the ones on your heart."

Mr. B stood up. Pointing his finger at Freddy's chest, he said, "You want to know something? God has already used you. He used you to help my son—yes, my own son Jake—while you boys fought those williwaws last winter. He used you to defend Joanie against a grizzly and He used you to defend her against Pete ... yes, I heard all about it. He used you to bring life and breath back into your sister, Mattie. And Jessica. Believe it or not, you're not only good at fishing and teaching others, you're good at saving lives."

Mr. B chuckled. "There's no end to how God has been using you. So forget the past mistakes, Freddy, and get on with the future. Ask God to help. You can count on His promises."

Freddy nodded, left the tent, and made his way slowly to the lone cottonwood overlooking Eagle Point. Hunched over at the base of the tree, he pondered Mr. B's words. His whole being screamed, "Don't believe him. It's not true." But ....

*Mr. B is right. All this guilt is eating me up. How can I live with it? I'm so tired ... tired of trying ... tired of being scared ... tired of feeling like a damaged salmon that's been tossed overboard.*

Scars. How could he possibly look past them? His lip scar was a constant reminder of kids teasing him as a youngster. The biggest scar of all was the image of Mattie lying lifeless in the pool. It was stamped on his brain forever. But did it have to be? All the other images that told him over and over he was to blame … did they have to remain, too? Could God really, truly get rid of them? Mr. B's words sounded impossible.

*How, Lord? How can You do it? Is it really as simple as letting You handle it?* Freddy rubbed his face with both hands. He had to decide. Could he let God handle his guilt and fear? Jake had cried out to God when their boat was sinking and everyone said God answered his prayer. Could He answer Freddy's, too?

He squeezed his eyes shut, wrapped his arms around his knees, and bowed his head. "God, I can't believe I'm talking to You," he whispered. "My head says You can't help. But my gut says to believe that You can. I'm sorry for putting You down, for believing I could handle things. I made a mess of everything. Never thought to ask *You* to help. But now I'm asking."

Freddy's voice gained strength. "If You can hear me, God, would You please, please take this monster out of my head? Mr. B calls it guilt. If that's what it is, I-I sure would like it gone. Guess You already know how I feel, huh? Like … like a big, ol' sockeye caught in a net. I can't pick it out. Will You? Please? Uh … thank You."

After many seconds, Freddy unfolded his body and wiped his nose on his sleeve. He looked out at the sea as if waiting for God to show Himself in some dramatic way. Like in a sudden, rogue wave. Or in a huge blast of wind. He waited. And waited. Nothing happened but he felt compelled to wait a little longer.

Then, as he sat in utter silence, Freddy began to feel the weight of an anchor leave his body. He began to shiver—not like skin shivers from the cold, but warm, inside shivers almost like a mild tickle. He felt an unbidden smile lift the corners of his mouth and, for the first time ever, he didn't feel the scar on his lip. What he did feel was a sense of peace. And hope. Before he realized, a low, slow laughter bubbled out of his lips. *Is it gone?* He reached up to touch the scar. *No, it's still there. But the ones in my head, inside me … they're gone!*

Freddy's laughter became words meant for God alone: *Thank You.* Yet Freddy wasn't ready to leave, to give up the overwhelming sense of peace he felt. He sat alone, enjoying the quiet. Clouds had formed overhead, but everything looked brighter—the water, the grass and wildflowers, the leaves … even the muted sky. Overhead, a pair of eagles screeched clearer, louder. The earth itself smelled sweeter.

Out of habit, he shoved his hand in his pocket. Feeling the lucky knife, he drew it out. For a long time he stared at it, rolling it from one hand to another. With a sudden grin, he said, "Don't need this any more, do I, Lord?" But something kept him from thrusting it into the trunk of the cottonwood.

When he left, Freddy ran up the hill to share his happiness. But he knew he first had to take care of a few things. Once back at the cabin, the solemn sight of Mrs. B could not diminish his new-found joy. He knelt beside her head, stroked it lightly. "I'm sorry, Mrs. B. Sorry for waiting so long to leave the lagoon. But I know you'll be okay. God's gonna see to you."

Mrs. B opened her eyes and smiled. "I know, Freddy, I know," she whispered. Nearby, Mr. B grinned and gave Freddy a thumbs up.

Freddy stood to face Bernie. He cleared his throat. "I'm sorry, Boss. I shouldn't have waited so long to leave the lagoon. The accident was my fault."

Bernie raised his hand, waved it feebly. His eyes watered. "No, Freddy, it was mine. I should have let you take the bigger skiff. Even though it's new. It would have gotten you through the inlet with no problem."

Freddy cleared his throat. "Uh, Bernie, there's something you should know. Something I hafta take care of. Uh, Pete's been killing seals. I seen … saw him twice. Thought I heard him other times, too. So … uh, guess I'll go talk to Uncle Hal. He'll wanna know."

Bernie's mouth tightened. His face reddened. "Okay, go take care of it."

Freddy left the cabin, refusing Jake's pleas to join him. Freddy had to do this alone. As he walked down towards shore, he saw that Hal, out a ways from shore, looked ready to come in any moment. *Good. I'll see Pete first and then tell Hal what he did.*

Before he got halfway down the hill, a piercing scream reached his ears.

## *Chapter 16*

# BEAR ATTACK

Freddy raced downhill when another scream sliced the air. Just beyond Bernie's skiff, a brown bear was attacking Pete. Without thinking, Freddy tore off towards the bear, shouting. "Hey! Get away from him! Beat it!"

As he ran, Freddy glimpsed a couple of good-sized rocks. He scooped them up, barely stopping. "Go on! Get outa here!" Close enough now to hear Pete's whimpers as he lay curled in a ball, Freddy threw a rock. The bear stopped moving its gigantic head back and forth. It turned around, saw Freddy, and huffed. But it moved away from Pete. Right towards Freddy.

His mouth dried to cotton. *He's gonna kill us both. But I'll get him. Lord, help me get him.* Anger instantly replaced his fear. In one smooth motion, he shouted again, threw the other rock, and drew the knife from his pocket. Click, he opened it and held it in front of his body. He spread his legs in a defensive stance, waiting. His heart boomed so loud, all he heard was its rapid beats.

The she-bear reared up, roared, turned around, and bounded up the hill behind Pete and Hal's cabin.

Sweating, panting hard, Freddy ran over to Pete. "You okay?"

Pete kept whimpering. His body shook like cottonwood leaves in the wind.

Freddy knelt beside him. "Let me see." He probed his cousin's arms and legs, but saw only one wound on his arm. "Here, Pete. Let me help you up. Looks like these scratches need tending."

Pete took a shuddering breath and cleared his throat while Freddy helped him to Uncle Hal's empty cabin. Pete slumped into a chair, leaned over the table. He pointed to the medicine chest.

"So what brought that on?" Freddy asked as he prepared Pete's wounds for dressing.

Pete mumbled, "Don't know. I was just walking."

Freddy studied the scratches. "They aren't deep, but this'll hurt." He cleaned them and swabbed them with antiseptic. Pete flinched but remained silent as Freddy wrapped a wide cloth around his arm and secured it with tape.

Once he regained strength, Pete's mood changed. He jerked out of his chair. "Leave me alone. I don't want you around."

Freddy's anger stirred. "You're welcome for saving your life," he spit out.

"Huh. That bear wasn't hurting me. Just checking me out is all. Now, get!"

Freddy stood his ground. "Yeah, right. You could've died out there. What's up with you? Has your nose grown so long, you can't see what's in front of it?"

Pete pounded the table with his good arm. "You and your … your friend Jake … just leave me alone! I don't want any half-brother."

"So that's it. You're jealous. Face the truth, Cuz. Whether you like it or not, he's your brother. Your *new* brother. What's it gonna do to your dad if you won't like him? Besides, what do you think God would say about that?" *I don't believe I said that.*

"Don't be giving me Bible verses. They aren't the truth, anyhow." Pete pounded the table again. Something popped out of his clenched fist and rolled to the floor.

Before Freddy could stoop to pick it up, Pete made a grab for it. Then Freddy remembered, through the haze of fighting the bear, that Pete's hand had been clenched the whole time.

"Let me see." Freddy forced Pete's fist open. "The skiff plug! So that's what you were doing down there. You jerk. Don't you have a decent bone in your body?" Freddy wrenched the plug out of his hand and took off for the skiff, praying it wasn't completely sunk by now.

Pete followed, running to catch up. "I didn't mean … I-I'll help you put it back. I-I'm s-s-s …."

Breathing hard while he ran, Freddy shouted. "You're sorry, all right. A sorry piece of crap, that's what. How can you be my blood relative … let alone Jake's brother? He's worth a hundred of you!"

Freddy stopped short, but only for a moment, as he realized the sudden change in his feelings. "Sorry, Pete. For my nasty words."

They reached the skiff at the same time and climbed in. It was already half full of water. Freddy groped around to find the plug hole. He shoved the plug in when he felt the hole under his fingers. He grabbed a five-gallon pail while Pete found a small container. As they bailed, Freddy caught a glimpse of Pete's face. He looked downright miserable. Freddy sighed. *I feel sorry for the guy. But I shouldn't. … Or should I, Lord?*

Pete pursed his lips, his face changing to determination. Grabbing Freddy's large pail, he thrust the smaller one at him. They kept bailing, breathing hard, grunting.

Freddy took a quick break to watch Pete. *He's a tornado! Scooping and tossing water right and left at twice the speed I can. In spite of his injury.* Freddy stood mesmerized. He felt like smiling.

Pete hesitated long enough to see that Freddy had quit bailing. "What?" he asked, obviously bewildered by Freddy's grin. Without waiting for an answer, he stooped to resume his frantic bailing.

Still grinning, Freddy followed suit. They worked in silence, Pete at the stern and Freddy at the bow. With each fill of the bucket, Freddy's anger and disgust deflated at the pace of a balloon losing air through a pin hole. Pete's motions became more relaxed, too. When they were almost finished, Freddy jumped out of the skiff and tilted it so Pete could scoop up the remaining water.

Soaking wet, they threw the pails back in the skiff and waded to shore. They shared spaces on Sitting Rock to dump the water from our boots. "Wow, do I need a shower. I stink like a fish cannery," Freddy said.

"Let's not say anything about this, okay?" Pete asked, cracking his knuckles.

Freddy shrugged. "Why did you do it?"

"I wasn't done getting back at Jake for taking my job last winter. The skipper promised me that job. When I heard he got it, I freaked. Couldn't get another deck hand job, so I was stuck doing nothing. Stuck not making money, either."

Freddy sighed. "How many times do I have to tell you? It wasn't Jake's fault that he got the job. It was sort of handed to him on a gold plate. The captain owed Jake's dad a favor. His dad is a chaplain, you know." Pete wouldn't like to hear that.

Pete stood up, balled his fists. "Well … you didn't have to become friends with him. I'm not gonna forgive you for that."

Freddy's stomach churned. *Not again. But I'm not gonna let his anger get to me.* He grabbed Pete's sleeve, jerked him around. They squared off, face to face. "I don't like you much when you bully people. But I ain't scared of you anymore. I've been learning some things lately."

Pete looked puzzled. He relaxed his angry stance.

"God says we need to love each other," Freddy continued. "The chaplain taught me that. And to forgive each other. I can hardly believe I'm saying it, but I forgive you, Pete. For punching me a good one. For cutting the holding line to Bernie's skiff. And-and even for teasing Joanie. But this forgiveness thing works two ways, Pete."

"What are you talking about?"

"Well, don't you think you should talk to Bernie? And your dad? They didn't keep you from getting Jake's job. Because of your stupidity, they lost a lot of time and energy. And money. And they lost respect for you, I'm guessing." Freddy got right in Pete's face and grinned. "Besides, maybe you'll make points with God, if you apologize."

Pete's face deflated faster than that pin-pricked balloon. His shoulders drooped until Freddy again felt sorry for the guy.

"God says I'm supposed to love you, Cuz." Freddy swallowed hard. "I'll try."

Pete jerked away, took a few steps towards his cabin. Freddy held his breath. *Am I pushing it, Lord?*

But Pete pivoted, stalked back to him like he was ready to deck him. He grabbed Freddy's arm and pulled him up the hill. "Let's get it done."

Freddy stumbled along, hardly enough breath in his lungs to keep a straight face. Was the guy really going to come clean? *God, if You pull off this miracle, I'll be a witness to the biggest scene of the summer. And summer's barely started. I can hardly wait.*

As they ran up the hill, Freddy marveled that he had earlier left the cabin feeling worse than when he faced those dreaded williwaws. *Maybe that's what Pete's been feelin'. Maybe I need to keep givin' him some slack.*

"Hey, wait up!" Hal yelled from behind them. "What's going on?"

Freddy pulled back, waited for Hal. "You're about to see a miracle, Unc. Come on in." Freddy and Hal followed Pete inside Bernie's cabin.

Mrs. B sat up on the couch, wrapped in a blanket. Joanie sat next to her on one side, Mr. B on the other with his arms hanging limp between his knees. But Freddy noticed that his color was good. He could hear Bernie and Barb talking to Jessica in the bedroom.

When Bernie walked out where the others sat and stood, Pete didn't hesitate. He looked like he could faint, but holding Freddy's arm, he stalked up to his dad, glared at him and then hung his head. "I'm sorry, Dad. I did you wrong."

The room exploded. Joanie hooted. Mr. B raised one arm, rasped, "Thank You, Lord!" Freddy and the others stood there with silly grins … except Bernie. The scowl on his face could have set a Kodiak bear running.

Hal wasted no time in grabbing Pete in a hug that would have done any bear proud. His eyes swam. When he closed them, they overflowed. Soon everyone else began to sniff and wipe their noses. But their grins remained. Except for Bernie.

Hal pushed Pete back but kept a death grip on his arms. "How did this come about, Son?"

Looking down, Pete scuffed his boots on the floor, his face still pale. "Well, uh … you see … Freddy s-saved me from a bear and … uh, he told me I needed to … the chaplain said …."

Mr. B interrupted. "Sounds like you and Freddy both have been wrestling with God. Right?"

Freddy grinned as Pete managed a slight nod.

"I'm proud of you, Son." Hal's voice choked, but Pete's face took on an unexpected glow that lasted all but ten seconds.

*Poor Pete looks like he wants to bolt. He's prob'ly not used to his dad's compliments. But by the look of his scowl, he knows he's not done yet. Poor guy.*

When Pete's face turned pink, Freddy bit his lip to keep from laughing.

"What's the big deal? I apologized, didn't I?" Pete scuffed his feet.

The room erupted in laughter. *Funny how we can laugh so hard and feel so good when our eyes are swimming. Must be God's way. Except Bernie's not laughing. What'll it take to loosen up the tight set of his mouth?*

Pete gave Bernie a funny look and turned to glare at Freddy again. *This has gotta be the hardest thing yet for Pete, I'm thinking.* Freddy gulped as Pete grabbed his shirt in a tight fist. The cousins stared hard at each other. Freddy refused to look away.

*Will he bolt now? I can smell his fear. Please, Lord. Don't let him give up now. Help him finish the job even if he hates me.*

Pete let go so suddenly, Freddy stumbled backwards against the door.

Looking as if he faced death, Pete scuffed over to Bernie. His hands clenching and unclenching, knuckles cracking, he lowered his head. "I'm s-sorry, Bernie."

A hush came over everyone as they leaned towards Pete, straining to hear his apology.

"I'm sorry about the skiff holding line. Will you … uh, will you f-forgive me?" Pete hung his head for long seconds and then raised it high. He looked Bernie square in the eyes.

Bernie stepped backward, his mouth opening in obvious shock. Pure disgust replaced his shock. Freddy wanted to puke.

Bernie glared at Pete and paced the floor, his fists tight balls. "You're a troublemaker, Pete. I don't want anything to do with you. And I sure as heck don't believe you. Now get out." He pointed towards the door.

Pete gasped. He turned to leave, quietly this time.

"But ... Bernie, he's trying to apologize! Aren't you even ...." Freddy quit talking at the look of disgust and disbelief on Bernie's face.

Everyone remained still. Freddy was confused. New feelings of pride for Pete battled with anger over Bernie's crappy attitude. How did it all fit together? God had helped him deal with his own anger and guilt. And God had to be helping Pete with his, too. But Pete was new at this forgiveness stuff. This love stuff. Would it survive Bernie's rejection of Pete's apology?

How could Freddy help Pete? Just the thought of wanting to help his cousin again surprised him. God sure had it right, how He could change a person's thoughts and feelings so fast. Freddy glanced over at Jake and Mr. B. They must have been reading his thoughts, for they both grinned. Mr. B said, "Amazing, isn't it, Freddy?"

But Bernie didn't seen to have a clue. He muttered about the closure being too long. He mumbled about the bad way his picnic turned out. He cursed Pete under his breath. The rest of the group sat like lumps waiting for ... what? Finally Bernie glared at Freddy. "What are you waiting for? We have to clean the nets."

Freddy jumped at the chance to leave the tension-filled room. But he would have liked more time alone ... time to untangle the events from his muddled mind. Time to savor the surprises of God's love and forgiveness. It wasn't like they had to hurry to clean nets. Tomorrow would be soon enough, before the next opener. But Bernie was on a mission.

Running to catch up to Freddy, Jake said, "What's eating Bernie, anyway? Here something good happens, and he's like a bear."

Bernie, already at the beach, hollered. "Hurry it up, boys. You're wasting my time."

They spent the rest of the late afternoon hosing down the nets. It took hours this time. Earlier, the salmon had been running faster than they could pick them out. They hadn't had time to clean the nets then. Now, jellyfish, seaweed, and ocean debris clogged them. While giving them a good cleaning, Freddy found lots of new holes. They finished cleaning right before supper. Tomorrow they would be patching nets.

Freddy almost hated to go back to the cabin. *Cleaning nets sure helped me zone out. Guess that won't happen in here. Feels like the air inside needs a good cleaning, too. It won't happen as long as Bernie's mad. Doesn't take much to upset him.*

After a meal filled with tension, Freddy, Jake, and Joanie left. Jake gave Freddy's arm a friendly jab. "Okay, what went on between you and Pete? God sure did a good thing, I'm thinking."

Not quite used to talking about God, Freddy flushed. But a grin followed. "Yeah, He did. First He dealt with me. Then it took a near-fight with a brown bear to get Pete to wake up. Even then, I had my doubts." Freddy shook his head. "Sure is a hard-headed cuss … but then, I guess I was too. Earlier, that is. I gotta admit, I was getting tired of him being down on you about you taking his job."

"Me, too. God worked out some of his kinks, I'm thinking. Even if he doesn't like me … and I don't like him much, either."

When Jake uttered those words, Freddy realized that during all of Pete's apologies, he hadn't looked at Jake, his new half-brother. Not once. *Wonder if Pete's off licking his wounds. I better check in on him later. Don't want this whole thing to backfire. Don't want it all to wash away like the tide.*

Jake interrupted his thoughts. "I just wish I knew what kinks keep Bernie hopping mad."

"Yeah, well, I know he went into debt for that holding skiff. Treats it like his baby. That's why he wouldn't let me take it to the lagoon. If he had, we wouldn't've had the accident. Probably making him mad. Feeling guilty."

Freddy looked at Jake. "Guess we can't do nothing …" He grinned at Joanie. "I mean, guess we can't do anything but wait till he comes around on his own."

"Guess so. Or wait till God brings him around," Jake said.

"Yeah. Like He brought you around. So … how are things with your mom and dad and Hal now?" Freddy squinted at Jake.

Jake kept his answer short. "They're taking it slow. It's all God's doing, like Mom says. And Dad … Wendall keeps reminding all of us about loving and forgiving."

Freddy decided to confess his own story about Mattie to his friends. But there would be plenty of time for that in the coming weeks. After all that had happened, he felt solid-sure they wouldn't ditch him as their friend. Besides, he wasn't about to keep any more secrets—regardless.

Joanie interrupted. "I'd love to keep walking … maybe go over to Hiding Rock with you guys. But do you realize nobody remembered to call about the bear? With all the excitement and all?"

Freddy frowned. "Yeah, I wonder why they keep hangin' around, anyway."

They all kept a sharp lookout as they hurried back towards the cabin.

*Chapter 17*

# INVITATION TO CHUGACH

Hal walked out of his cabin as the boys and Joanie headed uphill.

"We gotta call in about the bear, Unc!" Freddy yelled, his voice coming in hurried puffs.

When Hal caught up, he put an arm around Freddy. "A done deal, Freddy. Meanwhile, I want to talk to you about something. It's … wait a minute. Here comes Pete."

Joanie walked on ahead as Freddy and Jake waited for Pete to join them. Freddy was happy to see a half-smile on his cousin's face. But the smile left whenever he looked at Jake. *He can't still be mad at Jake! After I explained again about the job? He needs to cool off. Once and for all.*

"By the way, we had a heart-to-heart with Bernie," Hal said. "He'll come around, just give him time. But the reason I'm here is to … Jake, you could have blown me over with a feather when I saw your mom. And I know what a shock it was for you." Hal cleared his throat. "Uh … Jake, I know it's too early to call you Son, but I'd sure like to get to know you better. Are you okay with that?"

Jake nodded, solemn and silent as they all stood outside near the cabin door.

"I know you've had a rough time with Pete. Actually, so have I. After his mother died, he sort of went off the deep end. Right, Pete?" Hal turned to his son who shrugged. "Nothing I did seemed to help. And I already told him I was sorry for not always being there for him. But I guess after today, he's beginning to change some, too. Like the rest of you."

Hal addressed Pete again. "Don't know how it happened, Son, but when you 'fessed up to your crimes, it sure surprised me. I believe you meant those apologies."

Pete nodded this time. "I did, Dad. But Jake … he … I don't want …."

"Son, I know it's a shock learning you have a new brother. I know what you're thinking. He's going to replace you in my affections. But … much as I'll learn to love him, too, nothing will replace you. Understand?"

Pete hesitated, his gaze switching from his dad to Jake.

Hal continued. "It'll take some time, Son. But … anyway, I've been thinking. After the season's over, before you go back to college, Jake, would you like to do a weekend campout with me and Pete? And Freddy, of course. The Chugach mountains are great. I've fished for trout at several of the lakes in the park. It's a great place. Maybe we could head up there over Labor Day?"

Freddy whooped. He punched Jake. "Say yes! You'll love it."

Jake nodded. "Sounds good. Dad told me he's having bypass surgery in mid-August. He should be up and running by then. Yeah, that sounds like fun." He turned his gaze on his new brother and held up his hand. "What do you say, Pete?"

Pete stared at his hand for long seconds before cracking his knuckles. Freddy couldn't deny the scowl that persisted on Pete's red face even as he raised his hand to meet Jake's high five.

A wide grin spread across Hal's face. "Good. It's all settled then."

Hal's face grew serious. "There is one more thing to deal with, Pete. Those seals you clubbed? … Yes, I'm aware of it. And yes, I was horrified my own son would do something so cruel."

"But, Dad … I did it for you! Don't you …."

"I thought about it a great deal and realized you just wanted to make sure I wouldn't lose any more salmon than needed. And … " Hal cleared his throat. "… I realize I haven't been there for you when you needed me most. All those things you did … when your anger got the best of you, I should have stepped in and helped you deal with it.

"But getting back to the seal clubbing. You know I'll have to report it. We'll both be at the mercy of the Feds. But we'll hope for the best … that is, unless you do it again. Understood?

"Yeah, Dad. Understood. I was gonna tell you anyway." Pete's voice cracked. "Okay if we go home now?"

"Sure, Son. Guess I'm done here. See you boys around." Hal started to turn, but added, "Oh, by the way, a couple dead seals were washed up on the beach. My guess is that's why the bears have been hanging around."

As he and Pete left the group, Freddy couldn't avoid seeing the sneer on Pete's mouth as he turned to cast his narrowed gaze towards Jake. *Uh, oh. Pete's not gonna let go yet. I knew that high-five was fake. When is he gonna quit bullying Jake? What'll it take?*

As Freddy, Jake, and Joanie headed inside, Joanie met them at the door. Joanie poked Freddy in the back. "By the way, Fred, your grammar is coming along. You've even quit dropping most of your g's … you know, doin', seein', and other words."

Freddy agreed, happy to see Joanie's bright smile. "You're a good teacher, I guess."

"Yeah? Well, you're a quick learner. That's all it takes. Soon you'll be running circles around me with your own teaching. I can see it now. You're surrounded with thirty second graders, their eyes wide open as they listen to you read a story. Yep, you'll make a fine teacher. Better save up your money for college. Maybe online schooling, huh? Imagine! You can get satellite internet and go to school at fish camp."

Freddy closed his eyes, trying to visualize himself sitting at a computer studying. *Nothing's too hard for God, Mr. B said. I'll go along with that.*

"Hey, Sis!" Jake's words interrupted Freddy's dreams. "Can you believe we're going camping in the Chugach."

Joanie's eyes became slits. "Who's we?"

"Me and Freddy and Pete. Hal's taking us over Labor Day."

"You mean in the state park? Up by Anchorage? Seriously? I've always wanted to go there. My friends said the mountains and glaciers are gorgeous there … and all the wildflower meadows. Can I go along?"

"Sorry, Sis. This trip's for guys. Besides, Mom'll need you to help take care of Dad after his surgery. Maybe next summer."

Joanie sighed dramatically. "Once again, the fairer sex is ignored." She turned her gaze to Freddy. "Promise me you won't let my brother lose his journal in the lake while you're camping, okay?"

"Promise." Freddy gave Joanie a wink.

Jake snorted. "Yeah. I still don't know how you managed to rescue it before the boat went down last winter." His eyes took on a sheen.

"Earth to Jake, earth to Jake," Joanie said. "The Coast Guard saved your life, not the journal, Bro."

Jake jerked his head as if to remove cobwebs from his brain. "Well, I gotta admit, that journal sure helped me get through the crappy part of that fishing trip. Knowing I was writing for you, Sis, made me feel closer to home. Guess it helped me stay balanced … or focused … or whatever."

Freddy and Joanie shared a laugh.

"Right, Jake. Balanced," Joanie said. "Anyway, I'm glad Freddy rescued it for me. Sure glad I still have it, Bro. You will write in it on your trip, won't you? For me?" She batted her eyelashes.

"Of course, Sis." Jake wrapped his arms around her in a bear hug. "The williwaw winds of the Bering Sea almost claimed it, but the Chugach won't."

Freddy winked at Joanie while raising his thumb in a sign of resolve. "You can count on that, Little Sis. You'll see your journal again. Not even the wildest williwaw can change that."

CPSIA information can be obtained at www.ICGtesting.com
Printed in the USA
LVOW040959051212

310004LV00002BA/4/P